# Coyote Landing

By Jan Dearman

Beacon Publishing Group
ISBN (Paperback): 9781961504165

*Coyote Landing*


Cover Design by Jerry Parsons
Exterior Design by Lori Pace
Edited by Gerard Hernandez



Order at www.beaconpublishinggroup.com for a discount. Email to inquire about bulk purchase discounts at customerservice@beaconpublishinggroup.com

Beacon Publishing Group, New York, NY 10001
www.beaconpublishinggroup.com

Manufactured in the United States of America

*This book is dedicated to the beautiful "Cowboy State," which has been the source of many pleasant memories of adventures and people, including the late Virgil Horsely, the inspiration for the character, Virgil Garrison. Sheridan is the birthplace of our family's own special "Coyote."*

# Coyote Landing

# Chapter 1

"Ladies and gentlemen, we have just been cleared to land at Billings Logan International Airport. Please make sure your seats are in a full upright position and your seatbelts are fastened and remain fastened until the plane comes to a complete stop at the gate. The flight attendants are currently passing through the cabin to make a final compliance check and to pick up any remaining cups and glasses. Thank you."

Looking out the window, Jemma couldn't see the snow-covered mountains she remembered and loved. But only an hour and a half down I-90, she knew the Big Horns would welcome her back to Sheridan, the town of her birth and the destination where her dreams ended in the reality of working plans. She was thankful she had been able to sleep for a couple of hours during the layover in Dallas. Now her mind was whirling with schedules and tasks, but she knew she could rely on her neat organizer to keep her on track, if her cell phone and tablet should let her down. She knew she sometimes lost time and convenience in backing up technology with neat, carefully considered, written notes, but she found clarity and freedom in the security that gave her.

An experienced RN, having worked from Med-Surg to Natal to ER at University Hospital, Jemma now relished the idea of new challenges away from the familiarity of the Tennessee mountains that had been her home since childhood. Wyoming had been "calling to her," to something deep within her psyche, since her family's last visit to Sheridan when she was "almost a teenager." Now, nearly fifteen years later, she knew it was time to answer the call—really, to find some answers for what she wanted in life. She knew it wasn't another broken heart, even at the risk of losing the fading dream of marriage and children. She would do what she knew to do with the best of her nurse's training and proficiency—and let God take it from there. She remembered the Scripture, "A man's heart plans his way, but the Lord directs his steps." She thought with a smile: *I'll just keep moving forward and let God twist and turn the path as He sees fit.*

"Ladies and gentlemen, welcome to Billings Logan International Airport. The local time is 1:25 P.M., and the weather is a clear and pleasant seventy degrees. For your safety and comfort, please remain seated with your seat belt fastened until the captain turns off the 'Fasten Seat Belt' sign. Please check around your seat for any personal belongings you may have brought on board with you, and please use caution when opening the overhead bins, as heavy articles may have shifted during the flight."

When the seat belt sign went off, Jemma picked up her computer bag and put it on the seat. Waiting for a break in the aisle traffic, she moved to retrieve her jacket and carry-on from the overhead compartment.

"Here, let me get that for you," a man's voice spoke over her shoulder.

"Oh, thanks, but I can manage," she responded.

"No doubt, but I have to do a good deed every day, and I think I can count this."

Jemma grinned and moved aside, as a broad-shouldered denim jacket topped by a tan Stetson loomed over her to make quick work of retrieving the heavy carry-on. Five-ten in her stocking feet, Jemma wondered, *How tall is this guy?* "Thanks so much," she said, as he set the bag on its wheels, flipped the ID tag aside to retract the handle, and moved back to allow her passage to the aisle.

Tipping his hat, he replied, "No problem, ma'am. Welcome to Montana."

"Well, actually, I'm headed toward Sheridan. I was born there."

"Oh, a Coyote," he said, with the same two-syllable, long O pronunciation her Uncle Virgil used.

"Yep, so my uncle calls me."

"Well, guess you'd say I'm a Montana Grizzly. Either way, welcome home to God's country."

"Thanks," she replied, as she thought with a smile, *I wish I could see more of you than just those big dimples and sandy hair curling up under that hat!*


Jemma made her way to the baggage claim area, waited to reunite with her checked luggage, and reported to the rental car counter nearby. "I'm Jemma Garrison. I have an SUV reserved in my name."

"Just a moment, please," the petite brunette agent replied, as she entered information into her computer. "Yes, we have a mid-size SUV waiting for you, with an open-ended return to the Sheridan Wyoming Airport. Is that correct?"

"Yes, it is," Jemma answered, satisfied that she would soon be on the road to Uncle Virgil's, less than two hours away.

"I just need you to sign this form and initial where indicated. Also, if I could get a credit or debit card, a copy of your driver's license, and proof of insurance coverage, if you opt not to purchase coverage from us."

Jemma completed all the requirements, took the keys the lady offered, then asked, "May I leave my bags here while I go freshen up in the ladies' room?"

"Of course," the clerk replied. "Just put them there at the end of the counter. Would you like for me to have the car brought around to you?"

"Oh, that would be much appreciated." Jemma thought a five-dollar tip would be worth not having to lug her bags out to rental parking. Now, she was eager to brush her teeth, neatly re-braid her shoulder-length blond hair, and touch up her makeup. She wanted Uncle Virgil to see his grownup niece looking her best.

Jemma was pleased with the roominess and comfort of the vehicle, as she cruised at eighty miles per hour through the rolling grasslands bordering I-90. Miles of fenced ranch acreage, scattered trees and thickets, and the occasional settlement of dwellings and farm structures in the distance lined the route, which seemed free of any rest stops or amenities for weary travelers. Jemma was glad she had taken the time to freshen up before starting toward Sheridan, where she knew Uncle Virgil would be awaiting her arrival with tasty food, comfortable lodging, and a warm bear hug,

Reminded of bears—grizzlies, to be exact, she thought of the ursine good Samaritan who helped her with her baggage. Shaking her head, she rebuked herself, "No! No men in this woman's life right now!" Thinking of Cory still brought true heartache—and, yes, she knew it was simply the physical connection between the cortex and vagus nerve—but more than that, it was the disconnection of hope and dreams from the reality of a fraudulent, freeloading narcissist. Thankfully, she realized his nature and intentions before any commitment was made. After the break-up—supposedly reformed, he had returned to his old way of living just over the line from morality, legality, and human compassion. Jemma had emerged from the fog of love wiser, independent, cautious, and perhaps, cynical about relationships. Surely, she came from a family of what appeared to be happy unions, maybe, she thought, even providentially arranged. But, as she had told her sister, Laurie, if she ever encountered "the one," he'd have to be a godsend; and some divine messenger would have to thump her on the head, because her noggin would be buried deep in a protective hole.

Jemma saw the approaching road sign: "Exit 509, Crow Agency," and the word "Baaxuwuaashe" written beneath it. *How in the world would that be pronounced?* And she wondered if little Crow children had to learn to spell such words. She also noticed the same exit was the way toward Little Big Horn College. *Never heard of that. I'll have to look it up online.* She remembered the family vacation, during which she proudly turned thirteen, and their visit to Little Big Horn Battlefield. She laughed to remember Grandpa's watching for rattlesnakes as he quietly read historical markers, and her dad's sneaking up behind him to let out a blood-curdling war whoop. Grandpa would have had a heart attack had he been older and not so strong.

Jemma noted another sign announcing there would be gas, food, and restrooms at the Crow Agency exit. *I wouldn't mind a little snack and something to drink*, she thought. *I'm making great time with this speed limit.*


The trading post was convenient, less than a mile from the interstate. At the check-out counter, Jemma purchased a bottle of water, a stick of bison jerky, and a container of mint gum from a pretty, young Crow woman, who greeted her with a smile and "Good afternoon. Welcome to Crow Agency."

"Mind if I eat and drink while I look around?" Jemma asked.

"Oh, no," replied Tess, the name Jemma noted on the

girl's badge. "Are you here to see the battlefield?" she asked, referring to the site of "Custer's last stand."

"No," Jemma replied, "but I visited there many years ago. I'm on my way to Sheridan to see my uncle. I'm planning on moving to Sheridan."

"You have work there?" asked Tess.

"I hope to find a nursing position as soon as I get settled. I've been a registered nurse in Tennessee for several years."

"We need nurses here in Crow Agency. Maybe you could find something here."

Not wanting to be impolite, Jemma moved away from the conversation as she responded, "Well, you never know what the future holds."

The clean, fresh atmosphere of the store was calming, with colorful, organized displays of local crafts, interspersed with the requisite tourist supplies. As she drank water and grazed on jerky, she was attracted to the display of handcrafted silver jewelry. A black leather watch band trimmed with intricately tooled silver leaves and flowers caught Jemma's eye. She quickly persuaded herself that her watch, so vital to her nursing days, could use some "spiffing up"—*What more practical souvenir of my move could I find?*

"Tess," Jemma called to the salesgirl, "Could you help me? I'd like to get this watchband."

"Yes, Miss …?"

"Garrison. Jemma Garrison. Just call me Jemma."

"Yes, Jemma. That's been a popular watch band, the last one we have in stock."

As Tess took Jemma's payment and proceeded to wrap the purchase, the door chime sounded, and the women looked up to see a tall figure entering the trading post.

"Seth! What are you doing back here so soon?" Tess

called to the man.

"Got a call from the office on my way from the airport. Told me to just come on down here—the Rowletts' paint mare foaled this morning, and they need me to check 'em out. I was hungry and decided to stop on the way to pick up one of your good flatbread sandwiches."

Jemma noted the familiar form and dimples, and the sandy curls were completely exposed when the cowboy removed his hat and introduced himself. Combing his unruly hair out of his face with his fingers, he introduced himself: "I'm Seth Clay, veterinarian. Good to see you again, Miss Garrison." He laughed when Jemma, startled, asked, "How do you know my name?"

"Saw it on your luggage tag when I took your bag from the overhead. But I couldn't make out the first name— Jessie, Jenny …"

"Jemma, Jemma Garrison. You must be observant—and quick."

"Only when it comes to making note of a pretty girl," he grinned.

"I bet." Jemma tried to make her sarcasm biting. Turning toward Tess, she said, "Well, thanks, Tess. You've been really helpful. I've got to run." Nodding toward Seth Clay, she said, "Good afternoon … Mr. Clay." Jemma missed his questioning expression, as he looked at Tess, raised his eyebrows, and shrugged his shoulders.

In her determination to protect herself from involvement and potential hurt, Jemma often second-guessed her behavior. Perhaps the cowboy, vet—whatever he was, was simply trying to be nice, complimentary, but she had fallen hard for charming words and engaging manners that were nothing more than manipulation. Cory had known what to say and do to draw her into his newly reformed life. She, supposedly, had shown him the man he could be, the man he wanted to be—for her. *Yeah, right!* She had shown him job security, healthy finances, and a comfortable home—hers! She was an easy, attractive opportunity to freeload, while he, on the down low, maintained his bachelor pad with all the amenities, including a live-in girlfriend. Surely, not all men were like that—not her father, her grandfathers, Uncle Virgil. But all others now were marked with the same masculine potential for deceit and damage. *Never again!* she declared. She glanced at the speedometer and realized she was edging toward ninety miles an hour. *Get a grip*, she reminded herself. *You're still letting him control you!*

Searching for a radio station in Sheridan to divert her thoughts, she tuned to one offering  classic rock. They were playing Fleetwood Mac's "Go Your Own Way." *Can you believe that?* The Oldies station was playing ELO's "Don't Bring Me Down." *This is ridiculous!* The scanner finally settled on News Talk. Mindless to the discussion of current events disrupting the unity, peace, and security of the nation, Jemma allowed the drone of voices to bring her back into focus—getting herself together and finding her own peace and security in the open skies and fresh air of Wyoming.

# Chapter 2

Driving into Sheridan, Jemma thought it appeared like many other towns through which she had driven in Tennessee, though she knew Sheridan lay six times above the sea level of Chattanooga. The winters would be icy cold and snowy, as evidenced by remnants of March's last storm still holding fast to shadowed roof valleys and roadsides. A mixture of old homes, many now housing commercial establishments, fast food restaurants, and motels lined both sides of the street, eventually giving way to the older structures on Main Street that evidenced earlier times of rugged cowboys, dusty trail ends, and hotels with hot baths and soft beds.

Uncle Virgil's house was only four or five blocks off Main, and she was pleased to have her memory of the route confirmed when her GPS said, "In one quarter of a mile, turn right on Cleburn, then left on Kirkbride. Your destination will be on the right." Jemma welcomed the sight of the beautiful old home—sturdy, elegant, welcoming, having stood the ravages of Wyoming winters for more than a century. Her great-great grandfather Garrison, a young man who dreamed of cattle-ranching in the rugged northern state, moved there from Illinois to find that supplying ranchers was more profitable, with less investment of time, energy, and potential loss than raising beef himself. He built both his business and his house into structures toward which neighbors pointed with pride and appreciation for the benefit and beauty they brought to the burgeoning town. The family business passed into the hands of her great-uncle Virgil, when her grandfather, visiting "the Volunteer State" with an Army buddy, met her grandmother, married, and settled in the greener, if less majestic mountains of Southeast Tennessee. Nearly fifty years later, while her parents were visiting Uncle Virgil on vacation, Jemma was born—six weeks early, small, but fully-developed and screaming at full volume. Jemma thought, *I was meant to be born here, to call this place home.*

Jemma pulled into the double driveway and was not surprised to see Uncle Virgil descending the steps of the front porch, where he had been awaiting her arrival. As she exited the driver's side, she heard him shout: "There you are, my sweet girl! I thought you'd never get here!"

Jemma rounded the vehicle to embrace his lanky form and tiptoed to give him a kiss on the cheek. "It's so good to see you, Uncle Virgil! You're looking as handsome and healthy as I remembered."

"Well, your eyes must be seeing poorly, but they're as beautiful as the rest of you!" Releasing her to assess Jemma head to toe, Virgil declared, "My how you've grown up. You are truly a magnificent Garrison woman, and I wouldn't have expected any less."

Jemma giggled, shook her head, and responded, "Well, magnificent or not, I'll need some help unloading this vehicle. Put those Garrison muscles of yours to good use."

"We'll make quick work of it." Pulling bags from the open hatchback, he said, "I've got the whole upstairs ready for you. You'll have your own suite with living room, study, bedroom, bath, walk-in closet, and even a storage area. My neighbor, Mrs. Banning, has helped me get it ready. We've had a lot of fun fixing it up. She has a real talent for decorating, and I had the funds to underwrite the project. She's about run me ragged fixing, patching, painting, laying rugs, and hauling all her bargain finds and doodads.”

“Uncle Virgil, you shouldn’t have gone to so much trouble. I didn’t realize my coming would require such an undertaking.”

“Oh, no, no, I didn’t mean to make it sound like a burden. I’ve been so excited about your coming home to Wyoming, and I want to make your place here as comfortable and permanent feeling as possible.” As they ascended the steps and Uncle Virgil opened the door for Jemma, he whispered with a smile, “And between you and me, I’ve taken a real shine to having Mrs. Banning around.”

“Uncle Virgil! You’ve got a crush on your neighbor?” Jemma’s surprise was genuine—Uncle Virgil was well into his seventies.

“Well, when you meet her, you’ll see she is a fine woman—a widow for several years now. Her husband was a longtime surveyor around these parts—kind, well-respected, a good neighbor. A heart attack got him when he was out shoveling snow.”

“How sad. That’s not an uncommon occurrence in hard winter months.”

As they progressed through the foyer toward the stairs to the upper floor, Jemma noted the warm glow of oak flooring, extending throughout the house as far as she could see. To her right, a wide wood-burning fireplace, flanked by ceiling height bookcases lined the far wall of the living room, before which an assemblage of plump couches, armchairs, and ottomans enticed guests to put their feet up and stay a while before the warmth and crackle of the open flame. “This house is just the most gracious, welcoming place I’ve ever been—just as I remembered,” she declared.

"Well, I want you to know this is your home. This has always been Garrison property. Your granddaddy and daddy got themselves lost in the Tennessee woods, and now, it's time a Garrison came back home. You're a Garrison and a Coyote—nothing more to say," he laughed decisively.

Arriving at the upstairs landing, Uncle Virgil said, "That door to the left is a storage room with shelves and space for boxes and suitcases. Catherine even put a few plastic totes in there if you need them."

"Catherine?" Jemma asked with a grin.

"Mrs. Banning, you know. Catherine is her given name."

"Oh, I see," Jemma replied with a nod and a wink.

Leading Jemma to the door on the right, Uncle Virgil said, "And this is the door to your upstairs living quarters. I hope you will be comfortable and like what we've done. Change anything you want to change—it's yours to do as you please." Setting aside the bags he carried, he opened the door and pushed it so Jemma could enter.

Jemma almost gasped as she moved into surroundings that were everything she might have chosen had she been decorating the space herself. The tranquil softness of blue-gray walls enveloped the living area. A plush rug in pastel hues of blue, cream, and coral on the polished wood floor anchored a vanilla and beige striped loveseat with matching armchair and ottoman,  facing a gas log fireplace, with an ivory surround and mantel that extended to bookcases on each side. On the shelves were groupings of books, decorative storage boxes, and a collection of local native crafts. Above the fireplace a silver sunburst mirror reflected the amazement on Jemma's face and the wide grin of pleasure on Virgil's. "What do you think?" he asked.

"It's beautiful—absolutely beautiful! How did you

know—I mean, how did you know about the colors I like and … just everything?"

"Well … with calls to a concerned and cooperative mother and, like I said, a talented neighbor friend, I hope we've come close to meeting your taste."

"Oh, Uncle Virgil … meeting and exceeding anything I could have imagined."

Jemma continued into the adjoining bedroom, again a vision of soft, tranquil cream and blue-gray, elegant in its simplicity. Panels of drapes that matched the walls covered the windows looking out on the backyard and formed the backdrop for a queen size light oak sleigh bed with a tufted headboard. A creamy spread topped an assemblage of crisp white linens and beige and white pillows. Light oak nightstands holding sleek silver lamps with white shades were stationed on each side of the bed and matched the mirrored vanity table and chair on the right wall. There a lighted make-up mirror, a vase of pink roses, and a crystal bowl full of Jemma's favorite chocolate mints waited to welcome her.

Unable to restrain her emotions, Jemma embraced her uncle as tears glistened on her cheek. "Uncle Virgil, this is just the nicest thing anyone has done for me … ever!"

Uncle Virgil held her to his chest and stroked her hair. "Sweet Jemma, your mom told me you've had some deep hurt and disappointment in the last several months. It's time for some good things to come your way. You just open yourself up to a new life in the beauty of these wide-open spaces. Let the wind blow fresh in your heart."

Jemma pulled away and wiped her face. "Thanks, Uncle Virgil. I want this move to be a fresh start. You've been so good to let me come and to help me like this."

Virgil held her arms as he spoke to her directly. "Jemma, I meant what I said. This is the Garrison home. If you decide to stake a claim on your future in Wyoming, this house is yours when I'm gone. I've got no child of my own to pass it on to. My business will be going into capable hands, but this house is for a Garrison, and you're it."

"Thank you," Jemma whispered. "We'll see what lies ahead, but I know I would treasure this place … and I would pray I might fill it with my own precious memories."

"Well, enough of this teary, sentimental stuff," he ordered. "Come see your office space and the nice bathroom and walk-in you've got. You've even got drawers in the closet for your folded things." Jemma snatched a tissue from the box on the nightstand, dabbed her eyes and nose, and followed her uncle through the doorway into the remaining rooms.

## Chapter 3

At the foot of the stairs, Jemma turned right to cross a wide hallway leading one way to the master suite and the other, to two bedrooms each with a half bath. She entered the spacious eat-in kitchen to find Uncle Virgil slicing a beef brisket and a trim, petite, white haired lady, she assumed to be Catherine, cutting vegetables for a salad. Unheard and unannounced, Jemma stood for a few seconds and watched the comfortable companionship of the couple as they prepared dinner. They were an interesting pair—the sinewy lankiness of Uncle Virgil and the pixyish Mrs. Banning, whose head barely came to his shoulder.

"I do hope she likes it … and doesn't think I was being too presumptuous. It's her space. I've just never had the opportunity to fix up something pretty and feminine. For that matter, I've never fixed up anything masculine and 'Western-themed,' like I wanted for my boys." She laughed, "With them, I was barely able to stay ahead of dust, grime, and muddy boots. Design and decoration were out of the question."

Virgil responded, "I'm sure she liked it. It was almost …"

Jemma interrupted to declare: "Almost like you had read my mind."

"Oh, Jemma!" Catherine exclaimed, wiping her hands on a dish towel. "So good to finally see this lovely Garrison great-niece your uncle has been bragging about." Coming to extend her hand to Jemma, she added, "I'm Catherine Banning. Please call me Catherine. I hope you don't mind my intruding on your welcome home dinner. Your uncle asked me to join you and to bring rolls, dessert, and make a salad. So, I am really kitchen help, not an invited guest."

Jemma laughed, "Oh, it's great to meet you, especially so I can thank you for the beautiful apartment. Obviously, a thoughtful, talented woman had to be behind its design.

My suitcases are unpacked and put away in the storage area, and everything I brought has found its perfect resting spot."

"I am so glad," Catherine replied. I have not had so much fun in years and years. Your Uncle Moneybags here winced a little from time to time, but I came in right on his budget and ticked off everything on my list of 'To Dos' and 'To Gets.' By the way," she added, nodding toward her uncle with a grin, "Virgil gets credit for the flowers and candy."

Jemma replied, "You both get more credit than I could possibly repay. Thank you … so very much." Feeling watery eyes, Jemma changed the subject, scanned the kitchen, and asked, "Okay, what can I do?"

Virgil said, "You can set the table. I thought we'd just eat here in the kitchen. I might should have fixed up the dining room, but this is more comfortable." Pointing to the butler's pantry, secluded in a nook with the refrigerator, he said, "The plates and stuff are in there … silverware in the drawer. There's sweet tea in the fridge, soda, juice … pretty much whatever you want."

Catherine added, "The rolls are in the warmer in the oven if you'd like to get a breadbasket and load it up. Virgil, you have a breadbasket?"

"A breadbasket?" he asked, his expression blank.

"Yes," Catherine winked at Jemma, "a basket for bread. You put a cloth in it, add the rolls, and cover the cloth over the bread."

"I don't think so," he responded. "How about a bread bowl?" He took a steel mixing bowl from the dish drainer and a clean dish towel from the drawer next to him. Laying the towel in the bowl, he held it out to Jemma: "Here you go … a bread bowl."

"Well," Catherine laughed, "There you go." She returned to the counter to finish the salad and set it next to the lazy Susan on the table, as Jemma returned with the rolls. Then, Catherine followed Jemma to the range and, with potholder in hand, gingerly removed foil-wrapped baked potatoes from the oven.

When places were set and bottles of dressing and condiments were on the table, Virgil announced, "Ladies, the pièce de résistance." On a large, oval, pewter platter, Uncle Virgil had arranged tender, lean slices of Wyoming-grown beef brisket. Placing the meat in the center of the lazy Susan, he declared, "I may not know much about cooking and breadbaskets, but I can make the best brisket this side of the Mississippi and north of the Rio Grande."

Jemma inhaled and responded, "Oh, it smells wonderful, Uncle Virgil."

"Well, have a seat, ladies, and let's pray for this meal, so we can have a go at it."

With Jemma on his left and Catherine on his right, Virgil offered them his rugged, calloused hands and held theirs gently in his, as he prayed: "We thank you, our Father, for this meal, for Jemma's safe arrival, and for the company of family and friends. We ask your blessing on this food and thank you for the bounty of it. May it strengthen us to live for Thee and serve Thee the remainder of our days. In the name of Your Son, Amen."

When the last fork was laid aside, Catherine declared, "Well, that was one fine meal, Virgil. I thank you for allowing the help to stay and eat with you."

Jemma laughed, as Virgil responded, "Mighty glad you liked it," and then teased: "Jemma, have you ever seen such a pint-sized lady put away food like Catherine can?"

"Catherine must have a high metabolism like a hummingbird," she replied.

Defending herself, Catherine informed them: "I know nothing about metabolism. I just eat what I want, when I want, and don't fret or analyze. I figure the stress of worrying about fat and calories is what puts on weight. Calories burn more efficiently when the mind is relaxed … I say," she declared with a grin.

"Well, I'll have to check into the medical journals and see if anything has been written to that effect," Jemma suggested.

Catherine added, "Speaking of calories, how about dessert? I have something special for Jemma." She scooted her chair from the table and went to the butler's pantry, returning shortly with knife in hand and a cake plate holding a three-tiered dark chocolate confection garnished with Jemma's favorite mint candy.

"Oh, my!" exclaimed Jemma. "That's the stuff dessert dreams are made of!"

Catherine beamed with pleasure and said, "Jemma, how about getting us some small plates and clean forks? And, if you want ice cream, there's some in the freezer. The scoop I brought is on the counter."

Virgil lounged before the living room fireplace that was ready to be fired up to warm the approaching cold evenings of fall, as Catherine and Jemma tidied the kitchen.

"I think I've eaten more this one evening than in the last few months," Jemma said, as she loaded silverware in the dish washer.

"Well, you're a beautiful woman," Catherine observed, "but I think you could stand to put on a few pounds.

You're a bit on the thin side, and you'll need some insulation for our cold Wyoming winters."

"Well, thanks for the compliment. But didn't that model of your generation … Twiggy? … didn't she say, 'You can never be too rich or too thin?'"

"That was the Duchess of Windsor who said that. The king of England gave up the throne to become her *third* husband." They cackled with laughter, when Catherine added, "She must have had something more going for her than just bones!"

Jemma and Catherine, carrying a tray with cups of after-dinner coffee, joined Virgil in the living room. Jemma sat next to her uncle; and Catherine set the tray on the broad ottoman in front of them, picked up a cup, slipped off her clogs, and curled up in the nearby armchair. Jemma already was drawn to Catherine, a lovely feline creature enveloped in the plush warmth of the overstuffed chair, against the rich dark leather of which her white pixie cut gleamed. She was not a statuesque "Garrison woman," but Jemma had the impression Catherine was Wyoming-hardened and capable of holding her own in any situation. Also, Jemma thought one would have to be blind not to see Uncle Virgil was taken with his "neighbor"—on the pedestal he had placed her, she towered above any Amazon.

"Well, Jemma, what are your plans, now that you've returned to your Wyoming roots?" Catherine asked.

"I've made contact online and will set up an appointment with HR at the hospital. They have some openings in TCU—transitional care, and Med Surg, even some sign-on bonuses, it seems. An option might be some travel nursing. That pays well, but I'd rather be stationed here, rather than away for lengthy stays. And, of course, I want to be able to enjoy my beautiful apartment," she concluded with a smile and toasting her cup to Virgil and Catherine.

"That must be so satisfying," Catherine observed, "not only to have such a rewarding profession, but to know you're in demand just about anywhere you go."

"It does give me some sense of security and freedom. And not having my own family yet …" The sudden, intrusive thought of Cory gripped her chest. "… I've been able to save a little nest egg. I had thought I might like to travel some. Now … I've decided I'm a homebody—just wasn't sure where I wanted home to be, until I got this overwhelming urge to come back to Wyoming."

Virgil took Jemma's hand and said, "Just know, this always will be your home … as long as you want it."

Jemma knew her emotions were again on the brink of erupting into tears, when Catherine interceded: "Jemma, we need to get you geared up for wintry weather. You know, we're not like Tennessee, where you've got four seasons and you're just about tired of one when the next one arrives. As Virgil sometimes says, 'Here we've got two seasons—July and winter.' You've got women's boots and polar jackets still in stock, don't you, Virgil?"

"Sure do. Everything you need. And, of course, Jemma, you get the special family, closeout, end of season discount, plus fifteen percent," he chuckled.

"Oh, Uncle Virgil, you've done enough already. I want to walk downtown and see the shops on Main Street. I'll come by the store and check out what you've got, but I insist on just the regular sales price … plus fifteen percent," she teased.

"You can meet one of my sons while you're down there," Catherine added. "He's really an artist at hand-tooling custom saddles. Been with you what, Virgil … nearly twenty years?"

"Coming up on it. A fine fellow, and I think he's training that talented grandson of yours to follow him."

"How many sons do you have?" Jemma asked.

"Just two—Caden, who works for Virgil in the saddlery, and Ethan, who is a vet here in Sheridan. Thankfully, they took after their father—decent height, strapping men—not like their shrimp of a mother."

"Don't let her fool you," Virgil responded. "She's small, but strong as an ox—or, rather, in these parts, a bison," he laughed.

"Virgil, you really know how to flatter a woman— NOT," Catherine faked her displeasure. She rose, returned her cup to the tray, and said, "I hate to leave good company, but I've got a granddaughter coming to spend the day with me tomorrow and need to rest up—she's a livewire and a shopaholic."

"How many grandchildren do you have?" Jemma inquired.

"Three—Caden's Monty, who's a college freshman, and his daughter, Julie, who'll graduate from high school this coming year. Ethan's only son, Cal, is away at Montana State studying to be a vet like his dad."

As Jemma moved to give Catherine a hug, she said, "Again, Catherine, thank you so much for putting your expert touch on the beautiful apartment. And thanks for making this evening so special."

"You're very welcome, dear. I look forward to many more visits now that we're neighbors. You drop by my place anytime." Turning to Virgil, she directed: "Virgil, don't eat too much of that cake—you know you're supposed to watch your cholesterol."

"Now, you never mind, Catherine. I've got my own registered nurse right upstairs to see to me."

"Yeah right," she said as she approached the front door

and left Jemma the parting words: "Lots of luck with that!"

After Catherine's departure, Jemma moved to collect the tray and coffee cups. "Uncle Virgil, I see why you're so taken with Mrs. Banning—Catherine. Already it feels as if I have known her forever."

"Yep, quite a woman—a little bossy at times," he laughed, "but quite a woman—a good woman." He followed Jemma into the kitchen, drew a glass of water, and took a tray of pills from the window ledge above the double sink. Jemma added the cups to the dishwasher and watched as he opened the day's dosage of medication.

"If you don't mind my asking, what kind of meds are you taking? Just medical curiosity," she added.

"Oh, just a little something for this and for that. I can't remember the names. I just try to remember to take them."

"Do you mind if I take a look?" He handed her the pill case, and then she asked, "Do you have the bottles they came from?" He opened a drawer to reveal rows of medicines and vitamins.

Examining the bottles while hiding her concern, Jemma teased, "You must be a threat to rattle with all these inside you!"

"No, no," he joked. "I creak and grunt, but don't rattle. Comes with age and the territory."

"Well, now that I'm here, if you don't mind, I'll check to make sure you remember to take your meds. We want you to have a lot more years and territory to cover." Giving Virgil a kiss on the cheek, she concluded: "Now, I'll say 'Goodnight' and go upstairs to take a relaxing bubble bath and then sink into my comfy new bed."

"Good night, sweet Jemma. Sweet dreams. I'll be up reading for a while and then call it a day myself."

As she ascended the stairs, Jemma was aware of a

growing sense of purpose, even perhaps, of providential oversight of this move to Wyoming. She needed a clean slate, a fresh beginning, but Uncle Virgil would need care and companionship in the time ahead. She prayed his years would be many—that he and Catherine might enjoy the blessing of a long friendship—and maybe even more than friendship. But, for now, Jemma's training and expertise could ensure care that would optimize his health and strength. She had something to give him in return for the blessing he had been to her.

# Chapter 4

Tying her robe belt around her, Jemma entered the kitchen to the smell of fresh coffee and cinnamon and her uncle's greeting, "Good morning! How did you sleep?"

"Oh, it was like floating on a cloud! I haven't rested that well in ages." Checking her watch, she declared, "Seven-thirty … I rarely sleep that late."

"I thought you young people sleep till noon," he stated, as he plated a pan of sweet rolls and set them on the lazy Susan.

"Uncle Virgil, thirty is closing in on me faster than I care to think. I'm only young by your seventy-something standards," she kidded, as she poured a cup of dark coffee into the favorite mug a nurse friend had given her. Traveling with her from Tennessee, the mug had the picture of a blonde nurse with a hypodermic needle and the words, "This sedative will put you out of my misery."

Virgil suggested, "Why don't you go on out to the sunroom and enjoy the view of the back grounds. I'll bring my coffee and the rolls out there. Can I fix you some bacon and eggs?"

"Thanks, Uncle Virgil, but coffee and a cinnamon roll will be fine. I'm not usually a big breakfast eater. Besides that, I don't want you to feel like you need to fix for me. We'll work together on housekeeping and cooking—and when I get a job, we'll just have to play it by ear. Nursing schedules can be hard things to pin down."


Jemma relished the warmth of the sunroom, an expansive space with a wall of French pane windows looking out on the gently rolling hillside that formed the grounds behind the house. In the distance, she could see the Big Horns, snow-capped even now. Jemma thought, *At this moment, in this place, I feel at peace for the first time in a long time.* She sensed her memories of Cory were beginning to fade with the excitement of her new home and life. She wondered if the intense hurt she had felt was not so much disappointment with Cory, but with herself for being so vulnerable and unable to read him for what he was. She knew the experience had left her unsure of her ability to judge character. For now, she would maintain the determination not to expose herself to more potential misjudgment and heartache.

Virgil brought last night's tray, now laden with sweet buns, a thermal carafe, and napkins, and set it on the table between two cushioned wicker chairs. "This is one fine morning," he declared. "Last time you were here, you enjoyed sitting in one of those Adirondack chairs out under the big horse chestnut. You're a book reader, like me—that's a comfortable spot to be alone and read in warm weather."

"I remember," Jemma recalled.

"What are your plans for the day?"

"Well, I'll call HR at the hospital, to let them know I'm here—maybe set up an appointment. Then, I thought I'd walk downtown, do a little shopping. I'll drop by the store, if you're going to be in the office, and take you to lunch if you're available."

"Sounds good. I've got a favorite diner you need to try. I'm a fixture there most workdays. The food is simple, cheap, and delicious. You ever had a bison burger?" he asked.

"Maybe, last time we were here. I don't remember," she answered.

"Well, you'll have one today—and, let me tell you, it will

be the most delicious burger you ever ate—unforgettable."

"Okay, then, it's a date. Noonish?"

"Noonish," he stated. "I'll show you around the store while you're there. We've expanded a good bit. Of course, we've got the winter gear we talked about, but we've also got some nice lady's Western clothes and boots that would look mighty fine on a tall, slim blonde like yourself. Cowboys around here will be lining the sidewalks just to have a look."

"Now, Uncle Virgil, no talk of cowboys," she warned. "There's no time nor place in this girl's world for cowboys … or for men in general. You, Dad, and Grandpa are tried and true, but all others are just big foreboding, threatening question marks."

Virgil finished his last bite and drained his cup, then set it on the tray and wiped his mouth with a napkin. "Jemma, dear, I'm being nosey, but … what kind of man was this fellow that he could have hurt you so much you'd give up home and job to come to Wyoming? I mean, you are an answer to my prayers to have some family out here. Oh, I have a lot of friends, church family, and Mrs. Banning, of course," he said with a wink and a grin. "But there's nothing like knowing you've got kin nearby as the body grows old and cold." He continued gently, "I'm just so sorry your move was motivated by heartbreak."

Jemma looked at her cup for some seconds and wondered if she was ready to relieve herself of some of the anger and bitterness that were her formidable defense. She moved to empty her coffee into the nearby jade plant. "It's good for it," she stated, smiling at Virgil, before gathering her thoughts and continuing: "Cory was everything a woman might want—considerate, affectionate, charming, handsome. He loved me and my family—or so he said. We'd have long conversations about the future, goals, about the importance of a shared spiritual life … children. After family dinners, we'd go out and sit on the deck … till we were under the stars … share our dreams." Taking a deep breath, she continued: "I never once thought anything amiss when he'd forget his billfold and needed gas in his car—or when he'd ask if we could use mine, because his was running rough and needed to go to the shop. He'd even attend Sunday worship with us … and spend the night on Mom and Dad's couch, so we could get an early start on my day off, which, of course, I was all too willing to underwrite. You see, the monthly check for proceeds from the sales of his patent license on some machinery he'd supposedly invented always seemed to be late—or lost in the mail."

Jemma glanced to see Uncle Virgil was listening intently, his brows fixed in a questioning frown. "One night we talked about getting married the first of this year—making a life together … a 'lifetime of adventure.' He told me to think about it—not to rush. He'd be waiting … then we'd pick a date, go look at rings … celebrate." Jemma exhaled a long, slow breath. "Mom and Dad, even Laurie, were questioning me, tactfully, when things about the relationship seemed odd to them. But I was always ready to defend Cory to the nth degree … I guess they decided they'd just back off, see what would happen, and be there to pick up the pieces and sop up the tears if things went badly … which they were."

As she gazed toward the old chestnut tree, Jemma recalled: "A couple of days after that night, on my way home from an early shift, I stopped by his apartment to give him my answer—I'd been by there, but never in his apartment. I rang the doorbell, and a scantily-clad girl answered the door. I asked if I had Cory Mitchell's apartment, if Cory was there. She called toward the bedroom, 'Cory, sweetie, you'd better come see about this.' I asked, 'Who are you?' and she said, 'I live here, but I guess Cory didn't tell you about me.' Cory came from the bedroom and was obviously surprised to have been caught. Without another word from me, he began flustering, 'Jemma, I can explain. It's not what you think.' The girl cackled and said, 'That's the same song he sings every time. I'm sorry, honey, but you're not the first one he's conned.'" Jemma stopped with a sense of relief, of finality. "I can't believe I was such a naïve idiot!"

Uncle Virgil reached across the table to squeeze her hand. "No, Jemma, you were open-hearted and thinking the best of a man, who, apparently, was very practiced in deceit. Just be thankful it didn't go any further, that you did find out the truth before you made any commitment." Trying to lighten the moment with humor, he added, "Before you had to buy yourself an engagement ring and a celebratory dinner." It took a few seconds for the meaning of his humor to register with Jemma. Then they both burst into laughter—laughter that was full and honest and that had been absent from her psyche for months.

# Chapter 5

*What a glorious day!* Jemma thought, as she eased the SUV into curbside parking on Main Street. *I've got to check with Uncle Virgil about getting my own car and returning this rental ... maybe after I settle on a job.* Doing a quick calculation in her head, Jemma figured she could afford another week or ten days before the SUV would start maxing her transportation budget for the month's transition.

Jemma's first stop was the coffee bar—she knew a mocha latte would be the perfect accompaniment for her perusal of the shops along the way to Uncle Virgil's "Garrison Emporium." The name given to the store by her great-great-grandfather was optimistic in his time, but her great-grandfather and Uncle Virgil had continued the family's labor to make it now a wealth of merchandise worthy of the title "emporium."

Assessing window displays, Jemma passed by several "touristy" shops, until she came to the book and stationery shop, which drew her like a magnet. Throwing her empty coffee cup in the nearby trash can, Jemma reminded herself she had been frugal with this budget category—she would limit herself to one fiction, preferably a mystery by a local writer; one regional history, maybe something about the Crow Nation; and a few special cards to send to family and friends. As she walked from aisle to aisle scanning selections, she settled before a section offering several interesting titles. After she had investigated and returned to the shelf one, then another, and another, she came to *The Apsaalooke Nation, the People and the Land*. "That's definitely one I'd recommend," came a familiar voice over her shoulder.

Surprised, she whirled around to view the chest, then the dimpled face of the cowboy from the plane and the trading post. "Sorry, ma'am, I didn't mean to startle you."

Jemma's unthoughtful response was, "What are you doing here?"

Laughing, he answered, "I just came down to visit a friend. When I come into Sheridan, I always stop by here to see if there's anything I can add to my library. I have more regional history books than I do medical texts."

"Medical texts?" she questioned.

"Yes, I'm a vet, working out of Hardin … you likely don't remember … Seth Clay. I'm afraid something I said at the trading post may have offended you. If so, I apologize."

"Oh, yes … well … my nerves have been a bit frayed," she admitted. "I'm sorry I was rude."

"No problem. Copacetic." Tipping the brim of his Stetson, he added, "Well, I'll leave you to browse. Have a good day. Maybe I'll run into you here again."

Jemma watched Clay's lofty figure as he approached the checkout station, laid a collection of books on the counter, retrieved a few free bookmarks from the small nearby cowboy boot, and laid them on top of the volumes. The salesgirl appeared to be familiar with him, and they engaged in some friendly banter. *He's probably familiar to every female in Montana and Wyoming—or will be, given time and opportunity*, she thought with characteristic disdain.

Adding to the history book, Jemma found a mystery set in Wyoming and written by a local author. Then, she chose Mary Higgins Clark's last book, which she hadn't read, knowing it would likely bring a sleepless night. Finally, she selected a few cards with regional photos and proceeded to check-out.

"Good morning. I hope you found everything you wanted," the saleslady greeted her.

Satisfied with her purchases, Jemma replied, "Oh, yes, thank you. I'll definitely be returning from time to time. I just moved here from Tennessee, though I was born here … many years ago," she chuckled.

"Well, welcome home. I'm Sharon Langley. I hope you are very happy here." As she scanned prices, she added, "You might be interested in our local art gallery next door. There is a connecting entrance at the rear of the store—just past the periodicals, if you'd like to stroll through the display. It's small, but we have some beautiful pieces and some talented local artists who are gaining notoriety.

"If you don't mind holding my books, I'll take a quick look, thanks," Jemma replied.

Strolling through the art gallery, she was drawn particularly to the paintings of one local artist, Keeton Fox, whose paintings reflected the region and its inhabitants in muted earthtone watercolors Jemma found appealing. She rounded a corner in the gallery and came face to face with the simple painting of a horse's head that was almost identical to one she had done as a teenager, just after a visit to Wyoming, and she was reminded she had tucked the piece into the zippered lining of the suitcase she had checked. There was a perfect place to display it in her apartment, right above the desk in the office area Catherine had arranged.

Jemma continued toward the Emporium, passing what she assumed was the diner Uncle Virgil had mentioned. The sign on the window advertised, "Home of the Beast—Wyoming's Biggest, Bestest Bison Burger." She smiled to think of Uncle Virgil's chowing down on "the Beast"—*At least*, she thought, *it's lean, not full of fat and cholesterol.*

As she entered Garrison's, the evocative smell of leather on a background scent of winter pine, welcomed her with a sense of relaxation and a flood of warm memories of previous visits with Mom, Dad, and Laurie. "Good morning, Miss. Welcome to Garrison's. May I help you?" The sturdy auburn-haired lady who had been arranging the window display turned to greet her. "Oh, oh, yes," she continued, "I bet you're Jemma, Mr. Garrison's niece. He told me a tall, beautiful blonde would be coming to take him to lunch."

Jemma laughed in response, "Well, tall and blonde niece—not too sure about beautiful," she replied.

"Well, you can be sure … trust me," she declared. "I hope we can contact you about modeling some of our new line of ladies' apparel during the street festival in the fall. You'd be perfect. Most of us around here don't have the physique to best show off the clothes, if you get my drift," she joked, placing arms akimbo on the width of her hips.

Immediately warming to Uncle Virgil's saleslady, she laughed and extended her hand: "I'm Jemma Garrison."

"Connie White, floor manager. I've been with your uncle for more than twenty years now. He's a good man … a fine man to work for," she declared. "It's good to meet you and to have you here in Sheridan. He's in his office … all the way to the back … there's a sign on the door."

"Thanks," Jemma responded. "I'll look forward to seeing you again."

"Same here," Connie said, "Please look me up next time you're in."

"Will do." She started toward the back, then turned, "Oh, Connie, after lunch, I may be back to look at some cold weather gear—boots, parka … whatever I'll need for Wyoming weather … when I'm not in scrubs and clunky nurse's clogs."

"Great! I'll be here to help," she added, as she returned to the window.


Jemma passed through the lady's section and saw a rack of down-filled parkas and coats, noting some in her favorite dusty blue. She would check out those—and some cowboy boots, assuming they could be as comfortable as she had been told—and assuming they had her size, women's eleven. *Like Mother said,* she remembered, *exactly right for your height.* She winced at the thought of the euphemistic descriptions that had been directed toward her—"statuesque," "regal," even Uncle Virgil's "magnificent" … at least, she had outlived the pejoratives from childhood—"Giraffe," "Amazon," once even, "Statue of Liberty." Sometimes, she'd like to feel "normal," maybe even to be described as "cute," "delicate," "petite." Her sister, Laurie, was not short, but she certainly didn't rise to six-one in heels.

Jemma knocked on the office door and was shocked to have it opened by Seth Clay, who took off his hat with a sweeping gesture and announced, "Come in, Miss Garrison. Mr. Virgil awaits your arrival." Uncle Virgil was chuckling and wiping tears of laughter from his eyes.

"What are you doing here?" she asked sharply.

Seth responded, "This is the friend I came to see. Mr. Virgil and I have known each other for years, since I was a kid. I try to see him whenever I come down to Sheridan."

Virgil ordered, "Come in, come in, Jemma. Have a seat." He directed her toward one of the two chairs before his desk, and Seth sat again in the other.

"I hear you two have bumped into each other on a few occasions," Virgil informed her. "Seth called to tell me he thought he had run into you on the flight into Billings—he saw your name was 'Garrison' and knew that I was expecting my niece. It's funny how small this great big, wide-open, territory is!"

"Well, Mr. Virgil," Seth said, "I've really got to be on my way. I'm picking up some meds from Ethan and heading to Crow Agency early in the morning. We've got to check out some of the strays on the reservation—make sure they're inoculated if they're going to be running around with the kids."

"Good to see you, son," Virgil replied. "You sure you won't join us for a 'Beast'?"

"No, thanks, maybe next time. I've got some food in the truck. I'll eat on the way back." Rising from his chair, Seth put on his hat, tipped it toward Jemma, and said, "Good to see you, Miss Garrison. Hope you enjoy your stay in Sheridan."

Jemma, her mind whirling with the series of chance encounters, nodded and watched as Seth left, closing the door behind him.

After some seconds of silence, Jemma stated, "Well, that was unexpected."

Uncle Virgil stated, "That's one fine young man."

"Probably popular with the ladies, too, I suspect." Her voice had an edge of bitterness.

"Oh, he would be popular, if he allowed himself to be. He's a good man, Jemma. He worked for me during his last couple of years in high school—nearly four years altogether. He was a dependable, hardworking employee I could trust to get a job done and done right the first time." Virgil picked up his pen and began doodling on the desk pad in front of him. "Seth and the love of his life, Rachel, married right after high school. He worked to support them, and I valued him—looked to him like the son I never had. Then … Rachel got pregnant. They were going to have a son … name him after me … Virgil." He smiled, "I told him that was no name for a baby boy of this day and age." Jemma noticed Virgil's eyes became watery, as he continued. "During birth, Rachel's uterus ruptured, and she bled to death. Little Virgil didn't last much longer, only a couple of days in the NICU. Seth was devastated by Rachel's loss and never left the baby's side. He was there when alarms started going off and nurses came running, pushing him aside to get to the incubator. … They couldn't save the baby."

Jemma wiped the tear coursing her check, as her uncle added: "I thought Seth might well go out to the mountains and finish himself off. He was gone for a time. … Then he came back … said he was going to go to college in Montana. He'd always wanted to be a vet … he'd focus on that and try not to let the grief destroy him. He's up in Hardin, works a lot on the reservation. He drops by when he comes to Sheridan to consult with the veterinary hospital here, get supplies, whatever." Virgil looked directly at Jemma. "He's nearly as much mine as you are, Jemma. I know men are not high on your list, but please don't be rude to him. He's no threat to any woman—and no woman is a threat to get him ... not as long as Rachel's in his heart."

"Yes … I understand," Jemma replied softly. "I've been painting men with a broad brush, I guess, and that's unfair."

"Well," he lightened the conversation, "now that you've determined not to be a man-hating beast, let's go eat one—a Beast, that is."

Coming round the desk, Virgil hugged Jemma as she stood and said, "Love you, sweet Jemma."

"Love you, too, Uncle Virgil. I'll try to get my head on straight."

"Good. You've got too pretty a face for the frowns I've seen from time to time since you've been here. Be happy that the past is the past and the future is full of promise. Relish each beautiful days as it comes … and eat a 'Beast' with me as often as possible," he laughed.

# Chapter 6

Jemma was standing at the kitchen table, checking her tote bag for her day's necessities—billfold, checkbook, phone, planner, pen, documents folder, makeup bag, hairbrush. *This is ridiculous. I might as well pack an overnight bag.*

"What's on tap today, Jemma?" Uncle Virgil asked, coming into the kitchen from the sunroom to pour himself another cup of coffee. "Got time for some breakfast?"

"No, Uncle Virgil, I've got an appointment with HR at the hospital in half an hour."

"What about lunch later—maybe another bison burger?"

"I might be able to do that. I'll give you a call and let you know how the meeting goes … let you know for sure." Picking up the keys to the SUV, she dangled them in front of her and continued: "By the way, when you have some free time, maybe you can help me locate a reliable used car, so I can return this rental."

"Sure, but I might be able to do better than that. We'll see about it after lunch."

"Okay, thanks," she said, as she headed toward the front porch. "I'll check in with you."

"Hope all goes well," he called after her, as she opened the door on the day ahead.

"Miss Garrison, your paperwork is in order, your credentials and references are excellent, and your CEUs certainly speak to your interest and commitment. You simply will be required to file the application for endorsement in Wyoming and pay the fee—everything seems to require a fee—and then, we'll get you on the schedule as soon as possible. The hard part will be on us—deciding where we most need you."

"I'll be happy to work wherever, though I do have favorite areas … those more interesting and challenging."

"Well, we can accommodate you. We already have RNs who are content to avoid 'interesting and challenging.' You'll find that, though we're not a large university hospital, we must be ready to manage what sometimes seems more than our share of difficult cases. Life in Wyoming can be harsh and dangerous—we get injuries, accidents, and old codgers," she chuckled, "who won't seek medical service until they're about down and out." She continued: "Let's get that application for endorsement filed today, assuming you're prepared with the fee, and I'll see what I can do to rush it through. Maybe we can set up a couple of days of orientation for you next week, then get you on a floor."

"That sounds good," Jemma replied. "I'm settled into my apartment. I'll enjoy a little time to get my bearings around town and see some of the area, but I'm eager to get back to work—to be a real part of the community."

"I saw in your paperwork you were born in Sheridan. Welcome back home." Jemma looked at the name plate on the desk to remind herself she was speaking with Loretta Rowlett. *Where have I heard that name?* she wondered. "And I see you are living with your uncle, Virgil Garrison. Mr. Garrison is a public institution around here—well-respected."

"He's really my great-uncle, but yes, he is a wonderful man. He's happy to have a family member back near him in Wyoming."

Mrs. Rowlett took application papers from her desk file, attached them to a clipboard she handed to

Jemma, and directed her to have a seat in the reception area. "When you're finished with those, just bring them back to me with a check for the endorsement fee—oh, and another for sixty dollars for the background check. I'll hit the ground running to get things approved. You don't happen to have a copy of your current license?"

Retrieving the file from her tote bag, Jemma replied, "Yes, in this I have my license and work history—also, original grade reports, diploma, even class ranking and award in nursing school." She laughed, "I tried to come prepared."

"I should say so," Mrs. Rowlett chuckled. "Well, we'll have no problem at all. If you will give me the license, I'll make a copy of it to submit with the application, and we can get you a temporary permit good for ninety days." When Mrs. Rowlett returned the license to Jemma, she said, "Why don't you just check in with me Monday morning at eight o'clock to begin orientation."

Jemma answered with enthusiasm: "That's great, Mrs. Rowlett. I'll be here. You have been most helpful."

"You're very welcome, and I believe you'll be a great addition to our team."

Jemma proceeded to leave the office when Mrs. Rowlett called, "Jemma, just a moment." Jemma waited while Mrs. Rowlett took an ID badge from a drawer, printed Jemma's name and pass information on the insert, and offered it to her. "When you've completed the paperwork, just put the clipboard in the mail drop on my door. Then, you might want to look around the hospital. This ID will get you into most departments. You'll get a better idea of where you'd like to land, at least to start."

"Thanks, I'll do that. I look forward to Monday."

"Oh," Mrs. Rowlett added, "Blue scrubs if you have them."

"I do—that's what we wore at University." With a parting wave, Jemma closed the office door on her way out. In the reception area, she chose a comfortable loveseat, before which a coffee table was conveniently situated for spreading out and organizing papers. Jemma had enjoyed a week's break from work and would enjoy the remaining few days of "vacation," but she was eager to get back into a routine that would require the planning and purpose she needed to feel in control of her life. As she settled into the seat and organized paperwork on the table, she noted across the room near the stairwell a triptych of watercolor paintings of the Bighorns. *I wonder if they're by the same artist whose work was in the gallery. Nice ... very nice.*

Jemma was impressed by the cleanliness and organization of the hospital facility, some of which, she thought, had to be new. The nurses and staff she passed in the halls were friendly, smiling, if not also greeting her with a "Good morning." She determined not to intrude, but to observe the normal function of each unit she visited. Coming to the nursery, she viewed only two neonate cribs with infants, one a hefty, screaming boy—"Charlie," the name tag indicated, surely weighing at least nine pounds, and the other, occupied by a small, sleeping, olive-skinned infant with a full mop of black wavy hair—"Baby Girl Jane." If like Neonatal at University, the tag suggested she was not yet named.

A nurse in surgical gown and cap came from the adjacent room to check on Charlie and to ease his discomfort. Seeing Jemma on the other side of the glass and noticing Jemma's ID pass, she motioned for them to meet at the intercom. "Hi, I'm NICU nurse, Rena Milburn. If you want to come to the door just around the corner down there," she said, pointing with a gloved hand, "you can come in. We'll get you suited up and you can inspect our innards."

Jemma laughed at her use of the unscientific term and replied, "Thanks, I'd love to."

Rena showed Jemma around a compact, but state-of-the-art NICU, just off the nursery. "Right now, we only have two patients in here and the two babies you saw in the nursery. This chunky little guy," she stated, as she moved toward an open incubator, "is about ready to go home. His mother had gestational diabetes, and we wanted to monitor him for a couple of days, keep a check on his levels." Moving to a closed-box, Rena continued, "This little guy was impatient and came at thirty-five weeks, but he's doing well. His mom and dad come twice a day to visit him, and we hope to surprise them with a 'Come break me out of this place' call early next week."

Jemma followed Rena into the nursery, where the nurse swaddled Charlie and, placing him in Jemma's arms, ordered: "Feel this squirmy, long chunk of lead—nine pounds, thirteen ounces. His mother's a fragile-looking little woman, I bet barely five feet tall. The human body is 'fearfully and wonderfully made.'"

The phone rang and Rena said, "Hang on. I'll be right back."

While Rena took the call, Jemma held Charlie against her chest, gently swaying the baby until his fussing ceased and his eyes closed in sleep. When Rena returned, she whispered, "Well, you've certainly got the gift!" The nurse took the child and placed him gently back in his bed. "I think we just can't fill him up. He's always hungry. We may have to start plunging rice cereal down him like our grandmothers did," she laughed.

Jemma moved to the crib where "Baby Girl Jane" lay, content and unmoving. "What about this little princess?" she asked.

"She's a pretty little thing, like her mother. The young woman rushed into the hospital in the final stage of delivery and gave birth about ten minutes later. She indicated she was Hispanic, her name Maria, but she surely looked bi-racial to me. That usually means exceptional beauty. The mother disappeared less than an hour after birth. When a nurse went to check on her, she found the hospital gown with a note indicating the mother was leaving the child to Social Services and the statement: 'Can't keep her. Find her a good home.'" She sighed, "This sweet baby is healthy ... had a Combined-Apgar of sixteen," Rena replied. "Her mother seemed to be young and in trouble, but she left her in a safe place. Miss Jane's with us while waiting on foster placement."

"She has such a sweet, lovely face," Jemma said, as she stroked the baby's head with her gloved hand. "Look at that ... she's smiling."

Rena peered into the crib. "I'd say that's a look of pure pleasure and contentment."

Jemma smiled, then moved away from the baby, and said with finality: "Well, I appreciate your letting me look around. I'd better move on. I have a lunch appointment."

The nurse replied, "Jemma, I hope you'll request placement with us. We are short-staffed in a few areas right now, but I believe none more potentially consequential than here with these little ones. My co-worker took an early lunch break, but we stay close, because we're 'it' on this shift. Thankfully, we only have the four right now." She laughed, "But, we're still in peak birthing season. And this time next year, after folks have been cooped up with cold weather's indoor entertainment, we'll have another burst of spring and early summer babies! We simply can't remain understaffed."

"I'll consider it," Jemma replied, as she moved to the changing area. She sensed something had touched her, had stirred her, but she couldn't put her finger on the source or explain the effect it was having on her.

## Chapter 7

"Let me help you load all this stuff," Uncle Virgil offered, as he started picking up the bundles Rena had carefully folded and bagged.

"Thanks," Jemma replied. "I probably exceeded my clothes budget by a ton, but I'm happy with my purchases. You have some nice things."

"Well, glad you think so. Garrison Emporium is happy to welcome you as our newest customer … and, likely, the biggest spender," he teased. "Of course, you know you got a twenty percent discount, because we're counting on you to be the face and figure of Garrison's."

"I've never done any modeling before … but for a twenty percent discount, I'll give it a go." Gathering the remaining bags, they moved toward the door and the waiting SUV. "If I'm terribly uncomfortable," she grinned, "I may raise my price to a twenty-five percent discount."

"No problem," he grinned, "you'd be worth every percentage point." He closed the hatch of the vehicle and ordered: "Now, I want you to follow me home to unload all these packages. I've got unfinished business to discuss with you."

"Sure," she agreed, wondering what kind of "business" remained unfinished.

With the purchases settled in the apartment, Virgil said, "Come with me." He led her down the stairs, outside, to the garages at the end of the driveway. "What have you got in your budget for a car?" he asked.

"Well, I figured I might find a dependable used one

for, maybe, ten thousand."

Unlocking and sliding open the door to what Jemma thought was the unused half of the garage, Virgil asked, "What if I offer to take half that for this?"

Housed within the space was a shiny gray Subaru Forester that superficially looked in mint condition. "It's ten years old but, I promise you, in excellent running order—new tires, flawless interior, never wrecked or even dinged, except for a few light scratches that have been polished out."

Jemma, amazed at the offer, opened the driver's side door to inspect the interior. "It's simply perfect, Uncle Virgil. But don't you use it?"

"Not in months … except just to drive it around town a bit to make sure it stays in good running order. I've got my truck and a 'neighbor' who doesn't mind riding in it. I really don't need this vehicle, and it's not good just to let a car sit."

"Well, are you sure five thousand is enough? I know finding something these days for ten thousand might have been tough."

"I tell you what … five thousand, and you have electric garage door openers installed. I'm getting too old to pull on these. Come bad weather, we can just drive right in."

"Well, if you're sure, you have a deal." Jemma moved to give Virgil a hug and said, "I'm always needing to thank you for something kind and generous you're doing for me."

He squeezed her close and replied, "It's not without ulterior motives … bribing you to stay in Sheridan … asking you to be 'Miss Garrison Emporium.'"

"Oh, so now it's 'Miss Garrison Emporium'? No, thank you, Uncle Virgil. I'll model your clothes, but there'll be no titles … I draw the line at that!"

"Okay, if you insist," he relented with a chuckle. "I was just teasing—I knew you'd never go for something so corny." From his pocket, he retrieved a set of car keys and handed them to Jemma. "Get your bag. Let's return the rental to the airport. I'll drive it, and you take this one. Then, we'll go by the bank, I'll deposit one of your fat checks and sign the Subaru over to you, and then we'll see about garage door openers."

"Sounds like a plan," Jemma responded.

Before taking her place behind the wheel, she called out, "Uncle Virgil, thanks again. Love you!"

"You're very welcome!" he returned, "Love you too, sweet Jemma! Follow me—you won't need your GPS."

# Chapter 8

Determined to fill the weekend with pleasant activities before Monday morning's orientation, Jemma parked in front of the gallery. Having saved so much of her vehicle budget on Uncle Virgil's Subaru, she would revisit the Fox exhibit to see if there was anything she could afford for the apartment. The only change she wanted to make was moving the sunburst mirror from above the fireplace mantel to a wall in her office, where it would reflect the view from the window—the tops of the trees and snow in the coming winter, not a face of weariness as she came through the door after a grueling shift at the hospital.

Obviously, Fox had produced some fine pieces, at least in her amateur opinion. As she left the HR area in the hospital yesterday, she confirmed the triptych paintings were identified by the distinctive "KB" initials. She knew what she liked and believed she had an innate sense of quality, but she was far from understanding what made "good art" good. She liked the soft colors of Fox's depictions of Native Americans. *Impressionistic, but somehow very real in their communication*, she thought.

"Do you like his work?" a voice asked.

She turned to see a man, a couple of inches taller, who appeared to be … *What? Native American, Hispanic, bi-racial?* She replied, "Yes, very much. I like the muted earthtones."

"How do they make you feel?"

"Oh … well, I'm not sure, but I sense the artist is not a simple observer—he has respect, perhaps pride … even love for his subjects and the land."

"Yes, good. That's exactly right," he declared.

"Really? How do you know? Do you know the artist?"

Amused, he extended his hand. "I am the artist, Keeton Fox."

Surprised, Jemma shook his hand. "Mr. Fox, I am honored to meet you. I am merely a new aficionado, no artist or critic, but I was attracted to your paintings the first time I was in the gallery. I never expected to meet you in person."

"Thanks for the compliment. Knowing my work communicates what I want … that's just most satisfying." Straightening a frame, he asked, "Are you interested in one particularly?"

"Oh, I'm not sure. Each one has its own beauty … produces a unique reaction, I guess." Moving down the display wall with Mr. Fox looking over her shoulder, Jemma stopped at the end of the collection, then returned to "Village at Early Morning." Jemma said, "This one seems to have everything—the village, the horses, and the solitary figure on horseback looking over the encampment."

"This is a favorite of mine … and how does it make you feel?" he asked again.

"It makes me feel a bit sad, but hopeful. It's a new morning. He seems to be viewing the scene with pride … a sense of possession and purpose."

Clapping his hands together, he declared, "Exactly. You got it." He laughed, "You must be a mind reader … very perceptive."

"Maybe you just did a fine job of expressing yourself," she replied.

"I'd like to think so. Are you interested in buying a piece?"

Jemma observed the posted price beneath the frame and winced, "That's just a bit over my budget."

"If you don't mind my asking, what have you allowed in your budget?"

"Maybe … half that. I realize art is an investment, but I'm currently an unemployed nurse … until next week, I trust."

Taking a pen from his jacket pocket, Fox leaned toward the painting, marked out a number on the price tag and wrote over another. He stepped back, "Now, is that doable?"

"Mr. Fox, I can't allow you to do that … that's too much."

"No … Miss … ?"

"Garrison … Jemma Garrison … but I really can't accept that generosity … that gift. You don't even know me."

"Miss Garrison, I am so grateful for your appreciation of my work. Just knowing it will hang in the home of one who understands and appreciates my art will be worth the reduction. Besides, I'm on consignment here. I set my own prices."

"Mr. Fox, you are far too generous, and I should not let you do this." She grinned. "But I can't resist a good sale. I will hang it with pride above my mantel. When I come home worn and weary at the end of a shift, it will make me smile … and I will remember your kindness."

Again, he took her hand and pressed it between his. "Thank you. You have made my day." As he moved to leave, he added, "Perhaps I'll see you again. I come in from time to time to bring a painting and collect a sales check. Maybe we could get together for coffee."

"Perhaps, Mr. Fox. We'll see," she hesitated.

"Good … and call me Keeton. May I call you

Jemma?"

"Sure, that's fine … Jemma." She felt a sudden need to be cautious. This man was attractive, polite, a fine artist … but a total stranger … moving a bit fast. He appeared to be in his mid-thirties, interesting, kind … but she reminded herself: *Be careful, Jemma. You have a bad track record assessing men.*

"The gallery manager is occupied right now. I'll have it wrapped and waiting for you next door with Sharon," he informed her.

"That's fine. And thanks again, Mr. Fox … for your generosity."

When Jemma knew he had left the gallery, she proceeded through the rear access to the bookstore and browsed the shelves for a few minutes. At check out, she told Sharon Langley she was to pick up the Fox painting. "Oh, yes, Miss Garrison, Mr. Fox said it would be wrapped and waiting for you to pick up when you finish shopping— perhaps after lunch?"

"Yes, that would be nice.  Will you accept my check?" Jemma asked.

"Oh, yes. Mr. Fox vouches for you." Sliding an invoice across the counter to Jemma, she said, "I believe this is the price on which you both agreed?"

"Oh, no," Jemma gasped. "He took off another hundred dollars."

"Yes, he's very generous. He paid the gallery's commission directly and said to let you pay the balance."

Jemma thought for a moment. "Just a minute, please. I'll be right back." Jemma returned to the display wall, removed the tag on which Fox had marked the reduced price, and again went to check out. "This is the price Mr. Fox marked on the tag, which, I assume, had I not determined to buy the painting, would be the sales price for any interested customer who followed me. I will not pay any less than this price. You may refund Mr. Fox's payment … or whatever you work out with him—that's unimportant to me. But I will not be beholden to Mr. Fox, whom I only met this morning, for his excess generosity. I appreciate his fine work, and I have expressed my thanks. That's the end of it."

"Yes, miss, I understand … completely," the lady replied, with a faint smile. "Would you like me to forward your message to Mr. Fox when he returns?"

"Yes, I think that would be appropriate … again with my thanks" Taking her checkbook from her bag, Jemma added, raising her eyebrow: "And, again, with appreciation for the price reduction."

Taking Jemma's check, the saleslady looked at the name and said, "Thank you, Miss Garrison. May I say you are a very perceptive woman." With a wink and a nod, the woman put the check in the drawer of the antique register.

With a quizzical look, Jemma said, "I'll be back this afternoon to pick up the painting. Thanks for your assistance."

"You're welcome. I'll look forward to seeing you later."

As Jemma strolled down the sidewalk, she thought, *Perceptive?* She was intrigued with the cashier's words: "You are a very perceptive woman"—the same descriptive Keeton Fox had used. She might have some inherent good judgment of art, but the saleslady seemed to imply she was wise to be cautious where Keeton Fox was concerned. *Well,* she thought, *I'm pleased to have the painting, and meeting the artist makes it extra special. But, like I said, "That's the end of it."*

## Chapter 9

On the day of orientation, Jemma awoke from her dreams in the pillowy softness of her bed. It was not yet daylight, but she felt rested and ready to start on this new path. As she reached for the watch next to her bed, she chuckled to herself: *How strange—dreaming of the babies in the Natal Unit, so new and tiny, but speaking as if they were adults ... Charlie's voice gruff and demanding and Jane Doe's, clear and sweetly persuasive. What was it they were saying?* Already the particulars of the dream were fading.

She straightened the bedding and replaced the decorative pillows, as she wondered if her subconscious was trying to tell her something—but, no, the nursery was not the place for her. Days there could be filled with the hope and happiness of new life; but also, there were those times when life, if only attained with pain and difficulty, promised a future of misery and heartache. She was reminded of Uncle Virgil's account of the sadness in the life of Seth Clay. How terrible to have lost both mother and child in short succession, after what she assumed was months-long, joyful anticipation of simply—as she was reminded of yesterday's Scripture, increasing and abounding in the love and happiness of young marriage. Besides, honestly, she knew every child would be a reminder that the picture of home and family she wanted for herself was beginning to fade with advancing age and diminished opportunities.

Jemma entered the kitchen to the warmth and smell of fresh cinnamon rolls. "Good morning, Nurse Garrison!"

Uncle Virgil greeted her. Setting plates of bacon and scrambled eggs on the table, he ordered, "Take a seat and eat up!"

"Uncle Virgil, you didn't need to all this, but it looks and smells delicious."

"Just a good start to your day," he explained. "Coffee, juice, both?" he asked.

"Big coffee, little juice," she replied. "Thanks."

Placing the drinks before her, Uncle Virgil asked, "Are you excited about getting started today?"

"Well," she replied, "I'm not sure 'excited' is the word. I am ready to get back on a schedule and to feel productive again. The down time has been great—I needed some R & R. But now I need to stop spending money and start making some," she grinned.

Uncle Virgil included Jemma in the blessing he said for the food. "Thanks," she said softly, as she picked up her fork. "It's good to feel part of a family here in Sheridan—not just us, but the church family too."

"Yes, we're small in number, but I think our presence for good is felt in this community." He continued, "Jemma, if you aren't too tired at the end of the day, I'd like to treat us to a nice dinner—and no, not a Beast, but maybe dinner at the Trailhead Grill … a little 'Welcome to the Community' celebration."

"That would be nice, Uncle Virgil. I'm sure today won't be very tiring—just orientation. I should be home no later than six. Could we make it seven? That would give me time to change and freshen up."

"Perfect. I'll make the reservation."

Jemma passed the newborn nursery on her way to HR and stopped to see if there had been any additions in the few days since she had last visited. In her immediate line of vision, Charlie was gone—she assumed now at home. In his place another boy, Derrick, appeared healthy, swaddled, and sleeping peacefully. To the left, Bonnie, a little girl with a crest of auburn baby hair, was squirming and threatening to howl. And, to Jemma's right was baby Jane, lying where she had been for days now, awake and quietly blinking to focus on elements in her environment. Curious, Jemma could not resist the urge to press the call button to summon the nurse on duty to the intercom. She was pleased to see Rena Millburn enter from the NICU area. "Good morning, Jemma. Are you psyched and ready to rumble?" she asked with a laugh.

"Good morning, Rena," Jemma replied. "I'm here to get orientated—the rumbling likely will come before the week's over."

"Good to have you on board. I'm hoping you settle in with us—we need you," she reminded Jemma.

"We'll see," Jemma replied, continuing, "I was wondering why baby Jane is still here. I thought Social Services was picking her up?"

"We did too, but they're having trouble finding placement for a newborn. I don't know how long she'll be with us. Jenny Ragland is on this shift with me, and we try to give Jane as much cuddling time as we can, but she needs to have a real home and mothering."

"Well … okay … thanks," Jemma replied, her mind whirling in strange new directions. "I'll see you around. Have a good day."

"Thanks. Hope your week goes well," Rena said, returning to her duties.

Jemma was finished by four o'clock, but already tired and eager to go home to refresh and get ready for dinner. The path to her parked car led her past the nursery once again, and she was drawn to Jane's bassinet, only to find the baby missing. Pressing the call button, an unfamiliar face appeared and responded, "Hi! You must be Jemma. I'm Jenny Ragland."

"Yes, pleased to meet you, Jenny. I'm headed home but thought I'd check on Jane. I assume Social Services finally found foster care for her?"

"Oh, I wish," Jenny answered. "She had a check-up this afternoon. Rena is giving her a bath."

"Here she is," called Rena, as she entered the viewing area, carrying the clean, coiffed baby, swathed in pink softness. "Just look at this hair!" she said, pulling the swaddling blanket away from Jane's head. "When I washed it, all these curls appeared—so pretty." Noticing Jemma outside the viewing window, Rena said, "Hey, there. Want to come in and play baby dolls with us?"

Jemma paused for a moment and then replied, "Sure, I'll come around. I've got a few minutes." By the time she was gloved, gowned, and masked, the red-haired baby girl—identified as "Katie" on the bassinet tag, was screaming. Jemma moved toward her, but Rena said, "Here, Jemma, take Jane, and I'll see what I can do for this little vixen."

Jane was snuggling against Jemma's chest when Jenny handed Jemma a bottle and said, "Here you go. It's time for her feeding. Don't let that sweet contentment fool you. She can get cranked up like Katie if the bottle doesn't come soon enough."

Jemma settled herself in one of the nursery rockers and pressed the nipple to Jane's suddenly eager lips. The baby sucked without pausing while gazing at Jemma's face. The baby's expression seemed questioning, assessing—*intelligent observation*, Jemma thought with a smile. The bottle was emptied in short order, and Jemma moved Jane, setting her upright, supporting her body with one hand while rubbing her back with the other.

"She made quick work of that," noted Jenny. She had finished changing Derrick's diaper and was placing him back in the bassinet when Jane emitted a loud burp. "And there is her seal of approval," she laughed.

Jemma noted the time on the nursery clock and said, "I'd better get going. I'm going to dinner with my uncle this evening."

Rena admonished, "Right after you change Miss Jane's diaper, which should be …" Rena paused for the familiar whoosh. "Right about now. She's like clockwork."

Jemma completed the task, wrapped Jane in her blanket, and held the package of baby against her breast. Jane's dark baby curls brushed her cheek as Jemma relished all the sensations of new life—the warmth, the smell. Without warning, she was overwhelmed with an emotion unlike any she had ever experienced—a need, a longing. This baby had touched something innate and vital within her—something she could not explain, something she feared she could not assuage. She placed Jane back in the bassinet. "I've got to run. I'll see you guys tomorrow."

"Okay," Jenny replied. "Have a good evening."

"Yeah," Rena added, "Look forward to seeing a lot more of you."

Jemma didn't respond, making a quick retreat, throwing her hospital garb in the laundry basket at the nursery exit and picking up her bag from a nearby seat. As she escaped into the brisk air of the late afternoon, she threw her mask in the trash can. *What's wrong with me?* she wondered. She felt a compulsion to do … something … what? *Think, Jemma, think.* Was she on the verge of an opportunity? … a challenge? … a cliff? She checked her watch, then her phone. She had more than an hour before Uncle Virgil expected her home. She had to act fast—before she had time to change her mind. She wondered if this feeling of compulsion was sheer impetuosity … or some working of divine providence.

# Chapter 10

Sorting through the decisions she had made and trying to decide how to approach Uncle Virgil with her plans, Jemma made her way up the stairs to change for dinner. She had learned the Social Services building was near the hospital and had stopped on her way home, taking the chance she'd find someone still on the job. There had been no one at the reception desk, so she followed the main hall to an office door that was ajar, revealing a worker organizing her desk and putting take-home files in her briefcase. Jemma knocked on the door and a tall, slim brunette with a white widow's peak, looked up with the words, "Yes, may I help you?"

"I'm not sure," Jemma replied. "I'm Jemma Garrison. My uncle is Virgil Garrison. You may know him."

"Oh, yes, of course. I know him—not well, but he's a familiar figure around Sheridan."

"I mention him because I'm now permanently residing in the Garrison home here. I'm an R. N. at the hospital—or will be as soon as my orientation is finished."

"Well, welcome to Sheridan. I hope you'll enjoy your new home. I'm Stella Abrams, one of the social workers. How can I help you? I only have a few minutes before closing."

"I'll try to be quick then. There is a baby, 'Jane Doe,' in the hospital nursery, and I understand the department is having some difficulty finding newborn foster placement for her. I want to know what I have to do to be qualified for emergency foster placement in our home. As I said, I am a registered nurse with certification and experience in neonatal care. I can offer her expert care, financial support, and most of all … love." Jemma surprised herself when she choked on her words and tears welled up in her eyes.

Pausing her activity, holding her briefcase on her lap with one hand and file folders in the other, Stella Abrams smiled and leaned back in her office chair. "Someone has fallen in love with a baby. That's a look we often see on the faces of foster mothers."

Jemma laughed and swept a tear from her cheek. "Yes, I think you've nailed it—I've fallen in love with a precious baby girl. I need her as much as she needs a foster mother."

Stella Abrams deposited the folders in her bag and said, "Fostering is a big responsibility, but I'm sure you know that. You likely have completed a recent physical; but also, there would be a home check, a brief psych eval, and various required references. Given your background and family connections here, I think we could move all that forward quickly, if you have time to work with us."

"I can work my schedule with the hospital to allow for whatever is necessary. What kind of time are we looking at?" Jemma asked.

"Well, I am aware of the case of Baby Jane. We want to get her into a home ASAP. Thus far, we've had no one willing to take a newborn. I could try to expedite this, if all the requirements and paperwork were in order. But I need to warn you: one of our approved foster families may change their mind, and we'd be required to move her immediately. I really can't give any time estimate. Can you come back in the morning at eight so we can start the process?"

"Sure. I'll be here." Jemma stated. "Thank you."

"You're very welcome. I look forward to working

with you," Stella Abrams said, as she retrieved her handbag from a lower desk drawer and picked up her case. "Come on. I'll walk you out."

# Chapter 11

Jemma dressed in gray pants with a matching long vest and an ivory silk button-down blouse. Tucking a dusty blue floral scarf under the collar and sliding her feet into gray leather mules, she double-checked her make-up in the sunburst mirror and fluffed her hair, loosened from its usual braid. She dumped her tote bag onto the desk and transferred a few essentials into a tapestry clutch. Checking her watch, she realized she would have some minutes to spare, even though she had spent several assessing the space in her apartment for a baby bed and nursery chest. *Yes, we can make this work nicely*, she thought. *Now, to approach Uncle Virgil with the proposal.* But she had to be patient and wait for the opportune time.

As Jemma descended the stairway, Uncle Virgil was coming from the kitchen hallway. He glanced up at her, did a doubletake, and whistled. "Why, I didn't think you could get any more beautiful but look at you now."

"Aren't you the smooth talker, Uncle Virgil," she laughed. "It's been quite a while since I dressed for dinner—it's a nice change. And don't you look handsome," she observed. Virgil was wearing black dress pants, a starched white shirt with a silver bison head bolo tie, and a tan suede sport coat. "Thank you, my dear. My neighbor is coming over to join us this evening, so I thought I'd make an extra effort."

"Well, I can guarantee your 'neighbor' will be impressed."

"We've got a few minutes," Virgil said, checking his pocket watch. "Catherine said she'll be just a little late—she had to take her granddaughter home. But if she's not here to leave on time, she'll just meet us at the restaurant. Why don't you have a seat and put your feet up a while," he suggested, sitting in one of the living room armchairs.

Jemma thought this might be the opportunity she needed. "Uncle Virgil, I have something I need to talk to you about."

"Jemma, I hope you feel you can talk to me about anything."

"Well, this is something that could affect *you*—seriously."

"Okay, I'm intrigued," he stated, nodding for her to continue.

Jemma said a silent prayer for wisdom to find the right words. "There is a newborn baby who was left in the hospital nursery … a beautiful little Hispanic girl, who is now in the Social Services system … but they haven't found a foster home for her yet. I want to apply tomorrow for emergency foster placement. I would be completely responsible for her. I've checked—on my way to the hospital, there is a day care center that takes infants and has a great reputation online. Of course, on my hours and days off, she'd be with me … I'd take care of feedings and all the expense." Jemma paused, breathless. "What do you think?"

Virgil moved to sit next to Jemma on the loveseat. She noticed he had tears in his eyes as he took her hand. "Oh, Jemma, I am so proud of you—and so pleased. That's a wonderful idea. I'm happy and excited that we might have new life in this house—a baby!" he said, slapping his knee with her hand in his. "What's her name?"

Jemma tried to restrain her emotion, as she replied, "Right now, it's Jane—Baby Jane Doe."

"Well, we'll have to see about changing that. Can

we call her 'Melissa Jane'? Hope you don't mind, but I've always had a fondness for that name—Melissa, and since I intend to share her with you …"

Jemma laughed. "Whoa, Uncle Virgil! She won't be legally ours … but maybe they'll let us call her that, at least for a while. That's a lovely name."

There was a knock on the door; and Catherine, elegant in a black jumpsuit cinched with a silver belt, entered without waiting for an answer and closed the door behind her. "Good evening, guys. Hope I haven't kept you waiting." Noting their lack of response, she turned to see their unusual expressions and questioned, "What's going on? Everything okay?"

"Oh, Catherine," Virgil answered, "Jemma's going to see about getting us a baby tomorrow. Won't that be fun?"

As they entered the restaurant, Catherine concluded their discussion of babies and foster care: "My only word of warning is, think about what losing Jane will do to you. If adoptive parents are found, they will snatch her right out from under your roof." Jemma and Virgil had no response, but Jemma knew the truth of Catherine's words—even now, the thought of such a loss was painful.

"Good evening, Mr. Garrison," the hostess greeted them. "We have your room ready in the back, if you'll follow me." As they made their way past the entrance to the main dining room, down a long hallway, Jemma noted the 'Western elegance' of the décor. She smiled to wonder how some talented designer was able to make log walls and mounted bison and antelope heads seem so chic.

They arrived at a door with a "Meeting Room" sign, and the hostess signaled with a knock. Jemma was amazed when Connie White, the Emporium's floor manager, opened it to reveal a horseshoe table arrangement surrounded by Jemma's family and new friends.

Jemma exclaimed, "What's all this?" Through clapping and shouts of "Surprise!" her mom, dad, and Laurie moved from the head of the table to surround Jemma in a group hug: "We missed you, dear," her dad said as he kissed her cheek. "Oh, yes, very much," added her mother. Laurie laughed: "We had to get out here before y'all got snowed in and flash-frozen."

After a few moments, Jemma moved from the gaggle of family and looked for Virgil, who was standing behind them with his arm around Catherine's waist. Jemma noted their familiarity with a smile. "Thank you, Uncle Virgil. This is so special."

"You are welcome, but this was my neighbor's idea," he informed Jemma, squeezing Catherine more closely to him.

"No surprise there," replied Jemma, giving Catherine a hug. "Such a 'neighborly' thing to do," she teased.

"Come, let's sit down," Uncle Virgil directed. "I'm starving."

As Jemma and her family made their way to the head seats, she waved at the assemblage of church members at the far side of the table and, as she passed behind them, thanked Connie and Seth Clay for their surprise. They were sitting with unfamiliar people, whom Catherine introduced as her sons, Caden and Ian, their wives, and her grandchildren, Monty and Julie.

When they had settled at the head of the table, Virgil tapped his glass with a spoon and stood to welcome his guests and make some remarks. The hum of voices faded, and Virgil announced: "Thank you, family and friends, for joining us this evening. We are so pleased to have surprised our Jemma with this warm welcome back home. She was born a Coyote and now has returned to claim that proud title, along with the blessings of planting her feet in the soil of 'God's country.'" His words were met with more applause and a couple of coyote howls. "But beyond this 'Welcome Home' celebration, we have a surprise for all of you." He reached for the hand of Catherine, who was seated next to him, and asked her to stand by him. "This is my lovely neighbor lady—you all know her. I have asked her—and she has agreed, to leave the neighborhood and become my wife. This is also the celebration of our engagement." More applause, whistles, startled gasps, and murmurings followed, until Virgil motioned for silence. "Now, I have a special surprise for my sweet neighbor. I never really did the official get down on one knee thing— not as easy these days," he added, as the crowd joined him in laughter. "Let's see if I can do this." Virgil bent his knee and knelt with an affected groan. Taking a red velvet box from his pocket, he opened it to reveal an emerald-cut diamond and platinum ring and asked, "Dear neighbor lady, friend … my love, will you do me the honor of being my wife?" Though tears coursed her cheeks, true to form, Catherine responded, "I've already said 'Yes, Virgil.' I haven't changed my mind yet!" Without stress, Virgil stood to place the ring on Catherine's hand and held it as he gave her a delicate kiss. Again, the audience erupted into celebration.

Everyone enjoyed a superb dinner of bison steak, seasoned and grilled to succulent perfection, with roasted vegetables and baskets of assorted freshly baked rolls and muffins. When waiters had removed dinner plates and began replenishing coffees and teas, the door opened to the entrance of a cart laden with a sheet cake decorated with a scene of the Garrison home with the Big Horns behind it in the distance. Jemma was shocked to see the cart was pushed by none other than Keeton Fox.

Again, Virgil tapped on his glass to bring his guests to order. Motioning toward the artist, Virgil announced: "This cake was not baked—let me clarify that—but designed and decorated with the artistic expertise of Mr. Keeton Fox. I know Jemma appreciates his work, so I thought, *Who better to paint a cake for us?*" He chuckled, "It was his first such commission. He's done an outstanding job of representing the Garrison home and contributing to the celebration of our Wyoming family's expansion with Jemma and the future 'Mrs. Virgil Garrison.'"

Everyone laughed and cheered when Fox asked with a woeful expression, "Are you really going to eat it?"

Following dessert and coffee, guests mingled, moving around the perimeter of the room from klatch to klatch, buzzing with conversation, congratulating, questioning, often erupting into boisterous laughter. Returning from the ladies' room, Jemma was caught by Keeton Fox at the door. He took her elbow and moved her aside, stating, "I hope you've enjoyed the dinner— especially the cake. I can't take credit for the baking, but I want you to know every stroke of buttercream frosting was applied with a brush of great care and warmth."

"Oh, yes, Mr. Fox. Thank you. It was a beautiful creation—such a shame to demolish it. But it was delicious and much appreciated." She started to move away, but Fox held her and continued: "Please call me 'Keeton,' and I meant what I said about getting together for coffee … or dinner sometime. There are some other excellent restaurants in the area—and some interesting sites I'd like to show you."

"I'm sure that would be lovely, Mr. Fox, but my schedule is going to be full of my nursing duties and some other responsibilities I'm assuming."

Undeterred, Fox declared: "I'm very persistent, Jemma. I'll call next time I'm in town, and we can …"

"Excuse me, Keeton," Seth Clay interrupted. "Jemma, your Uncle Virgil said your mom and dad need to speak to you." Seth took her hand and pulled her away from the clutch of Keeton Fox, saying under his breath, "No lie, Jemma. They were asking your whereabouts. But I noticed Keeton had you corralled, and you looked like you needed saving."

"Thanks, Seth," she whispered. "You've redeemed yourself from every negative thought I ever had about you," she teased.

"That's good to hear. I have felt rather unfairly blamed for being of the same sex as the scoundrel who tainted your image of men—men other than your dad and Mr. Virgil, of course."

She had confirmation of her assessment of Fox, when Seth informed her: "Just a warning—from what I hear, Keeton Fox would do nothing to improve that image. He has a reputation as a womanizer—and you are one of the infrequent female newcomers to the area, who happens to be exceptionally easy on the eyes, if you don't mind my saying. I'm not trying to be flirty or slick or anything—just stating the obvious."

Jemma laughed at Seth's honesty and openness. "Well, thanks for the compliment. I've had some indication of his 'slickness,' as you say."

Seth deposited her at the gathering of Virgil, Catherine, and her parents. Laurie, Jemma noticed, was in pleasant conversation with a couple of young church members. She heard her dad responding, "We can stay a week or two, but Laurie may have to get back to work … so, the sooner, the better."

"The sooner, the better, what? Jemma asked.

"Our wedding ceremony," Virgil answered. "We thought we'd organize a small ceremony, so your folks and Laurie can be here." Pulling his fiancée to his side, he continued: "Besides, Catherine here is forever young, but I'm losing traction daily."

Patting his chest, Catherine reprimanded him: "No more talk like that. Every day with you will be blessing." Directing her words to Jemma, she asked, "Jemma, will you stand up with me? We're just going to have two attendants who also will be our witnesses."

"Oh, Catherine, I would be honored. Thank you," Jemma answered.

"Seth's going to be my best man," Virgil announced. "We'll put a few flowers around the church building, get this bunch back together, order up another cake and some punch, and make short order of it."

They all laughed when Catherine declared: "Virgil Garrison, that sounds about as romantic as your annual open house and clearance sale at the Emporium."

# Chapter 12

Jemma had called Loretta Rowlett to tell her she would be at the hospital by nine—that she had some business to handle at Social Services. Now, five minutes late, she was bounding up the steps to the building, throwing the door open, and crossing the polished floor to the reception desk. "Good morning, I'm Jemma Garrison. I have an appointment with Stella Abrams."

"Yes, Miss Garrison. Ms. Abrams is expecting you. You may go back to her office. She said you know the way."

"Yes, thank you." Jemma slowed her pace and caught her breath before knocking on the closed door.

"Come in, Jemma." Stella Abrams, her brow furrowed in concentration, was making copies and assembling a folder of papers. "How are you this morning?" she asked.

"Fine, thank you."

"Have a seat," Ms. Abrams directed. "Are you still determined to parent Miss Jane?"

"Oh, yes, and I have talked with my uncle. He's excited and eager to have her in our home. He's even given her a name, though I've told him she won't be ours legally. Perhaps, Social Services will cut him some slack and allow him to call her Melissa Jane."

"We'll see about that," Ms. Abrams said curtly. "There has been a complication. I learned first thing this morning, Jane has been moved into foster care with a family who determined they can make accommodations for temporary custody."

Jemma sank against the chair's back. "Oh … no"

was her only response.

"Jemma, buck up, hope is not lost. We'll get you approved for foster care and move Jane to your home as soon as possible. We have to wait the specified time for termination of parental rights of an abandoned child—only a few months, but then we can apply for legal custody." She closed the folder, wrote a name and number on the front, and handed it across the desk. "In the meantime, I want you to call Roger Burnham—his name and number are on the front. Make an appointment to see him as soon as you can arrange a time. He's an associate of ours—an adoption attorney. I already have contacted him to tell him you likely will be working with him on the *adoption* of 'Baby Jane Doe,' so he knows your application is specific for this baby and will be at the front of the line."

Jemma could not find the words to respond. She only nodded in agreement.

"Currently there are no applicants to adopt in our immediate area, but that's not to say there aren't those in other areas who'll be checking regularly for available babies. The unknowns concerning Jane's background, perhaps, will be a drawback for some, but … well, just get on this ASAP."

Jemma stood and said quietly, "Thank you, Ms. Abrams. I will. You have been tremendously thoughtful and helpful."

As Jemma turned to leave, Ms. Abrams added, "Jemma, don't be concerned about Jane. She will receive the best of care with this foster family. They are loving people—just not ready to assume long-term infant care."

"That's good," Jemma responded.

"And, Jemma, tell your Uncle Virgil, with prayer and time, 'Melissa Jane Garrison' will be your baby's legal name—at least until the day she marries," she grinned.

Jemma still had twenty-five minutes before checking in at the hospital, so she called Burnham's office to make an appointment. "Good morning. This is Roger Burnham. May I help you?"

"Oh, Mr. Burnham, I didn't expect you to answer the phone. This is Jemma Garrison. Stella Abrams said she had messaged you about my calling to make an appointment."

"Yes, Miss Garrison, she did. She is interested in expediting your application for adoption of Baby Jane Doe. Can we get together to discuss the requirements, the fees, and the adoption process? I know you're a nurse at the hospital. Do you have any day during the week when you can come by my office?"

"I'll arrange to work a weekend shift so I can take Monday or Tuesday off. Do you have any open times on either of those days?"

"I can see you on either morning at ten. I'll keep that hour open both days until you confirm which day you have free. Please let me know today, if possible."

"Yes, I will," Jemma agreed.

"In the meantime, Miss Garrison, be gathering copies of all your vital documents and financial records. They will be collected early in the home study process. But we will go into detail about all that when we meet."

"Yes, Mr. Burnham. Thanks. I'll check in with you later today to let you know about the appointment."

Jemma made a continual effort to focus and concentrate on the duties of the day—the last of her orientation. She was eager to tell Uncle Virgil about the change in plans. She had no doubt he would be pleased and would be "all in" with preparations for "Missy Jane." First, she would check with Loretta Rowlett about her full-time status and where she would be located, at least initially. Then, she would see if the nursing director would arrange a schedule so she could work part of the weekend and have a weekday off for dealing with the adoption process.

Mrs. Rowlett's office door was open, apparently awaiting visitors. Rapping on the door frame, Jemma heard, "Hey there. Come in, Jemma. Take a seat. I was expecting you. Are you ready to be stationed somewhere and into a routine?"

"Yes, ma'am, I'm ready if you are," she replied.

"Good. We've been impressed with your work ethic … attitude … not to mention, of course, your knowledge and judgment in your nursing duties. We could use you in several areas, but we have this proposal." She picked up a sheet and turned it toward Jemma, who tried not to show her surprise at the figures she saw. We'd like to put you in transitional care. As you see, that placement comes with a ten thousand dollar signing bonus. We can't promise much excitement or many challenges there, but if you would like to pick up a shift in ER occasionally or swap a light day in TC for a day in another department that's under-staffed, that would be doable. What do you think?"

"That seems more than fair and agreeable."

"That's good to hear. We'll get all this paperwork signed and filed, and you can check in with the nursing director about your immediate schedule."

"Yes, ma'am. I want to talk to her about taking a partial weekend shift, so I can have an early weekday off."

"I'm sure Celia Hogan will be happy to work with you and accommodate your scheduling as possible. Check in with her when we're finished here. Welcome aboard."

Before Jemma left the hospital, she called her

parents. "Hey, Dad, do you guys have any plans for dinner? … No? Great! How about letting me treat us all to Beast burgers down at the café? … No, I'll come to the house and make a quick clean up before we go. Tell Uncle Virgil to arrange to pick up Catherine, if she's free. … Okay, I will. See you soon. Love you, too."

Jemma could not remember the last time she had felt so much excitement and joy in living. As she made the five-mile drive home, she realized the bitter memories and repressed anger she had brought with her to Wyoming had vanished. Thoughts of Corey had disappeared somewhere between the Trailhead Grill and her meeting with Stella Abrams. When she tried to recall Corey and the former relationship, he was just a vaguely familiar face in the now-distant past.

Remembering she would pass by the day care center; she decided to stop and get some information. Her first impression was that the facility must be a mother's dream. Everything was clean and fresh, with a light scent of pine in the reception area. Jemma checked at the window of the glass-enclosed office. "Hello, I'm Jemma Garrison, a nurse at Memorial. If possible, I'd like to get some information on what you offer here, particularly for infants, and the cost."

"Yes, ma'am. I'm Nancy Haskins, one of the coordinators. Let me get a package for you that will contain all the details." While Jemma waited, she saw in her line of vision the main playroom, where decorations were forest-themed, with stuffed toy woodland creatures, even rideable bison, positioned here and there. One wall was painted with a scene of woods, with owls, deer, and smaller creatures hiding in the undergrowth, just waiting to be discovered by curious children. Play and learning stations were visible, some of which Jemma recognized as being Montessori-inspired.

"Here you go," Miss Garrison. "I think this will tell you what you want to know. What is the age of your child?"

Jemma hesitated, then answered: "Well, I'm only beginning the process of adopting an infant … right now, a newborn. I will need some help with care when I'm on duty at the hospital, but I really don't know when I'll have legal custody."

"Oh, that's so special," Miss Haskins replied. "When the time comes, I'm sure you'll be pleased with what we provide, particularly in the nursery. We have a limit of eight babies in infant care, with a ratio of two to one, babies to caretakers. Our "Grannies," as we call them, are older women who are licensed and have spotless backgrounds. They are exclusive to the nursery, unless one is temporarily covering elsewhere during the babies' nap times. Of course, we have a full-time R. N. on staff for any health issues or accidents that might arise."

"It sounds ideal for my needs—and the baby's. Perhaps I can visit again sometime, when I'm out of this nursing garb and disinfected," she chuckled, "and have a tour of the facility."

Miss Haskins replied, "That would be great. You are welcome any time. One of us is always manning the office and would be happy to show you around."

"Well, thanks, Miss Haskins …'"

"Please," she interjected, "call me Nancy."

"Well, thanks, Nancy. I'll look forward to seeing you again," Jemma said, as she moved toward the exit, feeling she had taken her first real step toward organizing a future with Melissa Jane.

## Chapter 13

After a shower and donning clean jeans, a turquoise plaid flannel shirt, and light quilted turquoise vest, Jemma felt refreshed and eager to share her plans with the family. She re-braided her damp, towel-dried hair in a neat French braid and applied only a bit of lip gloss—she didn't like applying and removing make-up once a day, much less twice. She put her billfold in a vest pocket and slipped her feet into her new Emporium cowboy boots. *They're comfortable*, she thought, as she picked up the Subaru keys from the basket on her desk.

Jemma found her parents, Charles and Rita, sitting on the loveseat in the living room. "Hey, sweetie," her mother greeted her. "Laurie's finishing up, and Virgil has gone to pick up Catherine. We were just checking out the famous 'Beast burger' online. It sounds threatening," she laughed, "but it's nutritionally sound." *Mother ... always health-conscious*, Jemma thought.

Her dad observed, "Apparently, Virgil is quite the connoisseur of the Beast."

"He eats the Beast for lunch just about every workday," Jemma informed them, as she sat across from them in an armchair. "Of course, he needs to leave off the fries. Maybe Catherine can help him make better choices when they're married. You know he's dealing with some heart issues—nothing major ... yet. But he needs to be careful about his diet and lifestyle."

Her dad said, "The Garrison men generally have good lifespans, but cardiac problems have been the primary factor in their deaths, unless they had accidents ... or got themselves shot ... or hung."

"Oh, Charles," Rita chided.

"Well, you know, this was the Wild West," he teased.

Ignoring his humor, Rita observed, "Catherine seems perfect for Virgil. I thought he'd never marry, especially at this advanced age, but they seem to be so happy—even young and in love," she chuckled.

"Yes," Jemma agreed, "they are good together … happy …hopeful."

Laurie entered the living room from the back guest room. "Okay, I'm ready to go slay the Beast." At the same time, they heard Virgil's truck horn sounding in the driveway— their signal to load themselves in Jemma's car.

Offering her keys to her father, Jemma asked, "Dad, you want to be our chauffeur? I can just lean back and relax."

"Sure thing," he answered, taking the keys. "Why not take advantage of one of the world's best drivers."

Her mother teased: "Really? We'll see if any of us can 'lean back and relax.'"


Charles Garrison drew in a big breath, exhaled, and patted his stomach. "I must say, that's about the best hamburger—Beast burger, I've ever had. Thank you very much, daughter dear."

"You're quite welcome, Daddy dear," Jemma answered.

"It's got my approval," stated Laurie. "Wish I could take one back to Stan, but it'd probably lose something by the time we got home."

"Stan?" Catherine questioned.

"Yes," Virgil added. "I haven't heard about him."

Rita said, "He's Laurie's 'latest and greatest.'"

"Oh, Mom," Laurie responded. Directing her words across the table to Virgil, Catherine, and Jemma, Laurie stated: "He's a good guy—a professor in the math department—a bit of a nerd, I guess, but kind, sweet …

and handsome, even with his glasses."

"We haven't met him yet," Charles stated with a grin, but his description sounds like Jerry Lewis in the old *Nutty Professor* movie."

"Charles Garrison!" his wife scolded him. "That's neither funny nor nice."

Jemma noticed even Laurie joined in their laughter. Their dad's sense of humor was no family secret, and her mother's shallow rebukes only added to the fun her dad brought to their gatherings. Occasionally, Mom's words were serious, if she felt there was any true insult or injury intended by his remarks. "Charles," she said, "why don't you and Virgil go moose hunting or something for a few days, while we women plan a wedding."

"They're not in season right now, are they, Virgil?" he replied.

"Nope, but how about antelope? I bet Catherine would like to hang a mounted head above the four-poster in what will be our bedroom."

They all joined in a boisterous outburst, while Rita simply declared, "You men!" When their laughter waned, Jemma's mom said, "No kidding, ladies, we need to get together to see what Catherine wants for the wedding and how we can help. And, Jemma, you'll need to find a bridesmaid's gown, if Catherine has thought about color and style."

Catherine asked, "Could you girls come over for supper at my house tomorrow evening? I'll fix a pot of stew and cornbread for the men to have at Virgil's, and we can do our own thing and make wedding plans—just have a girls' night."

"That sounds great to me," Jemma replied, with her mom and Laurie agreeing. "I can be there right after I get home and take a shower." Turning to her mom, she added, "You and Laurie don't have to wait for me."

"We'll wait on you to make any final decisions," Catherine smiled.

"I'll look forward to it—sounds like fun," Jemma said, before continuing: "Speaking of decisions …" She waited until she had the group's attention. "I have made a decision that will be news even to Uncle Virgil, who, likely, has told you about my proposed application to be a foster parent."

"I have," Virgil stated. "I think they're on board with us."

"Yes, if you're sure, dear," Rita seemed to question.

"Well, thanks, but I had some discouraging news when I went by Social Services on my way to the hospital. Baby Jane was placed in foster care this morning—just temporarily."

Catherine could not restrain an "Oh, no!" and reached for Virgil's hand.

Then, Jemma smiled, "It's okay. Once I'm approved, they can move her foster care to me, so that's good. But also, I am applying to legally *adopt* the baby."

"What?" Virgil interjected. "You mean she would be ours to keep?"

"If all goes well—with planning, preparation, and prayer," Jemma declared. "Stella Abrams, the social worker, said, if we meet all the requirements, 'Melissa Jane Garrison' can be her legal name until the day she marries."

"Oh, we'll surely be praying—and doing whatever we need to do to get ready," Virgil assured her.

Catherine added, "I'm sure we'll have to do some work to get the house ready. I hear there are safety precautions they require. And anyone living in the house will need a background check."

Virgil teased Catherine: "Think that criminal record of

yours will throw a kink in the works?"

Catherine replied seriously, "I don't know. That parking citation may have left an indelible spot. But I'd be more concerned about the speeding ticket on your record. I can only imagine how fast you must have been going to get a ticket on I-90!"

Charles Garrison spoke up: "Just think, Rita, we may be grandparents without the grief of giving our girls away to some scoundrel or some geeky professor." Jemma knew she had arrived at a new and better place in her life, when she was able to laugh with them, without hurt or hesitation because of Dad's reference to Corey. The birth of a baby girl and the unselfishness of her mother now promised light to the shadows in Jemma's memory, with renewed hope for greater purpose and possibilities in her future.

# Chapter 14

The wedding guests were seated, and Jemma now waited to make her entrance. She was amazed at how quickly the Garrison women were able to pull this wedding day together. All Uncle Virgil had to do, besides making the honeymoon arrangements in Billings, was show up, looking good, with license in hand—everything else was ready. With a warning not to "pull any funny stuff," Dad had done a masterful job of putting together a medley of contemporary wedding songs that, even without the context of the wedding, could touch the heartstrings and bring misty eyes. Mom had organized the simple reception in the fellowship hall of the church building, and Laurie was directing the wedding party. Catherine's sons waited in the hallway behind Jemma to escort their mother to meet Uncle Virgil, Seth, and the preacher at the altar—and Jemma knew she should begin immediately trying to maintain her composure.

Catherine had chosen for her maid of honor a steel blue midi dress with a matching fitted jacket. Thanks to Laurie's styling expertise, Jemma's braided hair was entwined with a matching silk ribbon, and her simple bouquet contained mauve and ivory roses with baby's breath. With a gesture of love and gratitude, Jemma touched the necklace on her chest. Catherine had given her soon-to-be great-niece a beautiful, thoughtful bridesmaid's gift—an exquisite silver locket, which, when opened, revealed the picture of a small, dark-haired baby girl, Melissa Jane. When questioned about how she had managed to get the photo, all Catherine would say, with a sly grin, was, "Connections."

The first poignant notes of "Turning Page" began, and Jemma knew it would soon be time to take her initial step down the aisle. A door opened, and the preacher led the way from the baptistry changing room next to the pulpit area, where the men had been waiting for their musical cue. Jemma thought she had never seen two guys look more pleased, proud, and handsome than Uncle Virgil and Seth, in navy suits, crisp white shirts, and mauve ties and boutonnieres.

"I've waited a hundred years …" was the cue for Jemma to begin her slow procession down the aisle. "… I'd wait a million more for you …" Jemma thought about the many years of Uncle Virgil's life—years he had waited, believing he would pass from this life without ever knowing the joy and companionship of marriage. "If I had only felt the warmth within your touch…" Jemma looked at Seth to see his eyes fixed on her and … she realized … what? She forced herself to look away and heard, "…only seen how you smile …" Jemma was almost at her designated spot. "… I would have known what I've been living for all along …" Jemma felt clouds of … emotion … confusion … like her mind was full of static she couldn't clarify.

"Your love is my turning page …" was the cue for Catherine's sons to walk shoulder to shoulder, preceding Catherine down the aisle—she wanted their escort, but not their physical support. She said she was coming to Virgil a mature, independent woman, who, with the wisdom and experience of years, had made the decision to give herself to him freely and completely. "Only the sweetest words remain …" Catherine entered the aisle behind Caden and Ethan and waited for the assembly to rise and for Virgil's gaze to seize hers. She was a glorious bride in a flowing ivory chiffon skirt that reached just below her knees. A beaded fitted jacket emphasized her trim petite form; and a floral bandeau with short blusher veil complimented the fresh curls of her short blond hair. "I surrender who I've been ..." Jemma focused her attention on Catherine, knowing if she looked at Uncle Virgil, she would see tears and her emotional resolve would break. And, if she again looked at Seth, she might lose concentration on her duties to the bride. "...what I've been living for." The final simple piano notes faded, as Catherine joined Virgil, handed her bouquet of ivory roses to Jemma, and took Virgil's hand.

After the closing prayer, the preacher announced: "By the authority invested in me as a preacher of the gospel in the State of Wyoming, I now declare Virgil and Catherine husband and wife. Virgil, you may kiss your bride." Everyone laughed when Virgil reached down, put his hands on Catherine's waist, and lifted her to meet his lips.

With a kiss on Catherine's check, Jemma returned to her the bridal bouquet, and the preacher continued: "And now, I present to you for the first time, Mr. and Mrs. Virgil McKinley Garrison. James Taylor's "How Sweet It Is" was cued perfectly for Catherine and Virgil to begin the recessional. As the couple reached the doorway, Seth, as directed, moved toward Jemma and extended his hand. She hesitated, then reached to accept his offer, and the words returned to her, "If I had only felt the warmth within your touch ..." She looked at Seth and wondered if he was hearing the words too.

# Chapter 15

Catherine and Virgil left the reception in his truck, freshly detailed and spared the misdeeds of even Charles' mischievous hands. Their throng of well-wishers shouted and waved sparklers in the gathering shadows of early evening. Jemma knew they only had a couple of hours' travel to their "fancy lodge" in Billings, as Uncle Virgil had called it, their base for fine dining and for touring the Yellowstone area, a mutually favored attraction. Uncle Virgil had told Catherine they could go anywhere she liked—Europe, the Bahamas, Canada. But Catherine wanted to stay closer to home. She had said, "Virgil, there's nothing that appeals to me now more than you and home. Besides, we don't need to take a lot of time—we need to get back and start consolidating our stuff in one place."

Jemma watched the truck disappear in the distance and suddenly felt … maybe, a little bit lonely. Her parents and Laurie would be leaving in a couple of days; and Garrison House would be quiet, sad, and empty without Uncle Virgil there. She shivered as a cool breeze brushed across the back of her neck, but a warm navy suit coat suddenly wrapped itself around her shoulders. "Here you go. Maybe this will help. Evening chills start early these days."

Jemma looked up at the sound of Seth's voice and smiled at the sight of his dimpled grin. "I bet you were a cute kid," she stated.

"Where did that come from? A cute kid?"

"Yes, the dimples, the curly hair … you probably haven't changed a whole lot … just maxed out in size. How tall are you anyway? I don't usually have to look up so far to most guys."

"You are one weird woman," he teased. "But, yeah, I was a cute kid—at least, in my school pictures. And I'm six-seven. It's nice not to have to look so far down on you. How tall are you?"

"Five-ten in stocking feet which, by the way, are just the right size for my height, my mom says."

Seth chuckled, "So, they're kind of big, huh?"

"What do you think," she inquired, extending her recently pedicured foot with its heeled jeweled sandal.

"Nice toes," he responded … "kind of long." And they both laughed at their silliness.

After a moment's silence, Seth asked, "Would you like to get some dinner, or did you fill up on wedding cake?"

"No, in fact, I only had some punch—and, yes, dinner would be great. But let me go help clean up first, if you're not in a hurry."

"No problem. I'll see if I can move tables or something. If nothing more, I can just flash my charming dimples."

Jemma retorted. "Who said anything about 'charming'?"

Seth laughed, put his arm around her shoulders, and guided them back to the reception area. Jemma was struck by the natural ease of the gesture. She smiled to herself: Uncle Virgil had said Seth was like a son … *Makes us what … first cousins once removed?*

As they entered the fellowship hall, they found Mother and Laurie scurrying around, cleaning tables, and sweeping the floor, with the aid of a few ladies of the congregation who wanted to assist. Charles, having loaded the Subaru, was entering through the side door with the question, "Anything more to pack in the car? We're about full."

Rita answered, "No, don't think so. I'm going to put some of the flowers in the auditorium. They'll still be fresh on Sunday. The others I'll take to the house, or Jemma might even take some to the hospital."

Jemma apologized: "Mom, can we help? I'm afraid we were either too slow or you all were in high gear—looks like everything is back in order."

"Oh, no, dear—you were not slow. We're just organized," she declared with a grin. "I'm taking dishes and silverware home to put in the dishwasher—and tablecloths will go in the laundry at the house. The top tier of the cake is packed for the freezer. The rest, if these sweet ladies don't take it, I'll put in the fridge at home for you guys and Laurie to have later. Your dad and I are absolutely finished with wedding cake."

"Speak for yourself, my dear," her dad scolded.

"I'm speaking for you and your doctor, who said, 'Lay off the sweets,'" she responded.

"Oh, what's he know?" asked Charles, as he winked at Jemma.

Laurie interjected, "Jemma, we've got it together here. You and Seth are free to go your own ways."

"Well, if you're sure …" Jemma began.

"We are" was Laurie's flat response.

Seth said, "Mr. and Mrs. Garrison, Julie … I'll be headed back to Hardin tonight. If I don't see you again before you leave, it was a pleasure meeting you. I'll pray you have a safe trip home. And now that Jemma's here in Sheridan, I'll look forward to seeing you again."

Charles came to shake Seth's hand. "Hope we'll see you sooner than later."

Rita placed a sack of soiled table linens on a table and moved to give Seth a hug. "You take care of yourself, Seth. We understand now why you've been so special to Virgil."

"Thank you, ma'am. He's special to me too." As he and Jemma moved to leave the fellowship room, Seth turned to wave and said, "God bless you!"

"You too," came their response. Jemma noticed Seth looked directly at Laurie, who gave him a "thumbs up," in what Jemma wondered was some private communication between them.


"This food is delicious," Jemma declared, after her first few bites of beef curry. "How did you know Indian food is a favorite of mine?"

"I asked Laurie. Little sisters are a major source of valuable information."

"I bet. I caught that 'thumbs up' when we left the fellowship hall."

Seth wiped his mouth with his napkin, then remarked: "'I bet' … that's what you said to me that day at the trading post—shortly before you said, 'Good afternoon … *Mr. Clay.*'"

Jemma sighed, "I apologize … in retrospect. I was not in a good place when I came to Sheridan."

"Yeah, I know," he responded. "Virgil told me you were still trying to get over a bad experience with a guy he called 'a charlatan and a scoundrel.' The way he said it made the guy sound like nearly the devil himself."

"For a time, I thought he was … the devil himself," she grinned. "Now, thankfully, he's just a distant meaningless memory. Of course, it took drastic changes—leaving home, family, and work, settling in Sheridan. But there are times when I think the whole thing—the failed relationship, the relocation—was providential. I believe I'm where I'm meant to be."

"I hope that's the case. Maybe providence is working on my behalf too," he said softly, as he reached across the table to touch her arm.

Feeling the slightest twinge of hesitation, Jemma,

motionless, looked at his hand and said, "Maybe …"

Seth withdrew his hand to pick up a piece of naan. "I'm sorry. That was premature. I haven't dated, or even been interested in dating, for a long time. I'm ignorant and clumsy."

"No," she countered, smiling. "I'm still a bit gun shy."

They laughed together when he said, "Well, this potential relationship may go nowhere fast. 'Ignorant,' 'clumsy,' and 'gun-shy' aren't very positive descriptions."

Jemma hesitated, then said smiling: "No, there're not. But I think we might be able to work our way out of negativity."

"Good," he declared, handing her a piece of bread. "Here, you got to sop the sauce."

Accepting the bread, Jemma asked, "Has Uncle Virgil told you about my application for foster care?"

"Foster care? No, he hasn't. Tell me," he encouraged.

"Well … there was a beautiful Hispanic newborn signed over to Social Services by her unwed mother. She was left in the nursery until they could find foster placement for her." She noted Seth's expression of intense interest and listening, then continued: "She had such an effect on me … I can't quite explain it. But I knew she needed me, and I needed her. I couldn't stand the thought of her lying in that bed with only the arms of a nurse to hold her …  to comfort her … when time allowed or needs necessitated." She sighed: "Anyway, I was going to apply for emergency foster placement, but a previously approved family took her." Seth remained silent, as she continued, "So, now, I am applying to adopt her. If plans come together and prayers are answered, I will be mother to Melissa Jane Garrison before the end of the year. Uncle Virgil has named her already." Jemma stopped and waited for his reaction.

"I remember … the nursery." He was wistful in the recollection. "Now, it all seems like a dream … the shock, the grief … the waiting by the incubator, praying … the tears that wouldn't come, then came in such torrents I couldn't control them."

"I'm sorry," Jemma said, "I didn't intend to cause you sadness. Uncle Virgil told me about Rachel and the baby. I was thoughtless to remind you."

"No," he replied. "It's okay. At times, snatches of memories and feelings arise, but the particulars have faded. I, too, had to move away for a while—to get some perspective, to focus on a new goal … I had my life—our life, all planned. But a big period-full-stop, was stamped right there and then. I had to either put a full-stop on living or determine to move forward—inch by inch, it seemed at times. I determined to honor the lives of my wife and child by making something of my life—and, if I didn't, I'd have nothing worth giving to God in the end."

"You're a wise man, Seth Clay," she said.

"No, but I'm working on it." He was quiet, then said, "By the way, I think what you're doing is a wonderful thing. Melissa Jane will have a great mother—and a great family with all you Garrisons.

They looked at each other with affection and compassion. Then, picking up a piece of naan, she ordered, "Here sop up the last of that sauce."

# Chapter 16

Jemma entered the kitchen and found her uncle and Catherine sitting next to each other at the kitchen table. "Good morning, dear," greeted Catherine. "What a beautiful morning we have to start our family life together!" They had returned the previous evening from their week away in Billings. And, though Jemma was pleased to see them, she felt she might be an inconvenience or intrusion on the newlyweds.

"Have you got a few minutes?" Virgil asked Jemma.

"Sure. I have the day off and nothing on tap that can't wait."

"Get yourself a cup of coffee," he directed, "and join us for a ham biscuit. Catherine's are the best."

When she had settled at the opposite side of the table, Virgil said, "Jemma, Catherine and I have discussed our living situation quite a bit over the last several days and have come to a conclusion we hope you'll find agreeable."

Jemma feared she now might be an uncomfortable third wheel but was silent as she sipped her coffee and waited for her uncle to continue.

"Catherine and I had talked about moving all our stuff under one roof—this roof, but she's decided she wants to keep her house, for the sake of her children and grandchildren—so many memories there. Since the Garrison home was going to be yours anyway down the road, we thought I'd move in with her and finalize your possession of this house. We'd be near each other to visit and to help, Catherine's children would be pleased, and I'd be happy knowing this home had survived another generation. What do you think?"

"If that's your reasoning, I'm relieved. I thought you might be uncomfortable having me around—your being newlyweds," she smiled. "But Uncle Virgil, you don't have to give me the house now."

"I know, but think about it, Jemma. Won't your possession of this house look good on your financials for the adoption? This house is a part of Sheridan's history, and you are a Garrison and its rightful owner when I'm gone—why not now? I'll be nearby to help with upkeep—even taxes, if needed. But you'd have a sizeable net worth to show—and a stake in this community, with a reputation and family name to uphold. Surely, that would be a consideration when the adoption petition comes before the judge."

Jemma considered his words. "I understand what you're saying. I guess that's right, though it all sounds rather superficial. It all should be more about love and care and the ability to provide. I've got those."

"I know—and likely a house and name are superficial, even materialistic," he agreed, "but I'm sure a judge would consider them."

Another thought came to Jemma: "I could move my living arrangements downstairs and make a proper nursery on this floor, which would be necessary, I'd think, to pass the home inspection. My beautiful upstairs apartment could be a guest suite, until Melissa was older and could have her own 'big girl' space."

Catherine looked at Virgil and stated: "I hadn't even thought about that. We need to have a baby gate made that will close off the apartment but still look nice on that beautiful stairway."

"I've got just the fellow who can do that—a fine

woodworker and carver," he responded.

"And, Uncle Virgil, it may be that, since you aren't living in this house, you won't have to have background checks and provide vital records and financial documents. I think those are only required of those living in the home."

"That ought to speed up the process," he said. He paused, then continued: "Jemma, if Catherine and I were not going to be practically across the street, I would feel differently. But this is a good move for everyone. Just let me assure you, I have loved having you in this house—you've been a joy and a comfort. When I become your neighbor, I assure you, I'll make myself a nuisance, especially when our little Missy Jane arrives."

Jemma reached across the table taking a hand of each of them. "I hope you know how much I love you both. When Missy Jane is ours, I want you to be the favorite people in her world … you'll give her a family and show her love …" Jemma grinned "… and make terrific biscuits and cinnamon rolls …"

"You can count on it," Catherine declared. "And we love you, too … very much."

"Okay, enough," stated Virgil, threatening to become emotional. "Catherine and I will start moving my stuff to her house. That'll mainly be clothes, toiletries, office files … a few keepsakes—things we can just box up and carry over in a couple of loads in the back of the truck. All the furniture, most of the decorative stuff, even the kitchen equipment stays—you can keep it, sell it, or give it away … whatever."

"Oh, Garrison House needs to keep the original furnishings, though I may rearrange some for the sake of the baby. And I'll keep your master bedroom fixed up for the times when Uncle Virgil and Aunt Catherine stay over. I'll make the guestrooms on the other end of the hall my bedroom with the nursery next door—maybe even make an adjoining doorway and enlarge a bathroom to accommodate a tub for the baby."

"That's a great idea," said Catherine. "We could start that project right away." Jemma noticed Catherine's hesitancy before continuing: "May I ask a favor?"

"Of course," Jemma replied. "Anything."

"Would you let me help decorate the nursery? Having only sons, I never got to do any decorating for a little girl, and my daughter-in-law did her own thing without wanting help."

"That would be wonderful," Jemma assured her. "My apartment is beautiful proof of your ability—I know the nursery would be exquisite."

"I don't know about that," Catherine chuckled, "but it would be filled with love—imagination … and fun."

Virgil interjected: "We need to get on all this today. Catherine, we'll get boxes and start loading up my things. We can leave most of the boxes in the back of the truck until you determine where you want to put me and my stuff." He grinned and squeezed his wife's hand. "Also, I'll make a few calls and get men lined up for the remodeling. Jemma, I'm sure you have a list of things to do today but think about exactly how you'd like the layout of the bedroom, nursery, and bath. We need to have all this completed by the time of the last home visit—maybe they'll give you some idea about the time frame."

"Okay … well … wow. Give me one of those ham biscuits. I'm going to need a lot of energy to keep up with you guys."

# Chapter 17

Jemma was leaving Stella Abrams' office, having learned Mrs. Abrams had requested official assignment as social worker to Baby Janes's case. There would be a home study in the next couple of weeks and at least two or three more in the next few months. She said she was staying connected with Roger Burnham to coordinate the process, which, if all went as smoothly as possible, might be completed in ninety days, depending on a court appointment.

Before putting her keys in the ignition, her cell rang, and she answered to hear Seth's familiar voice. *Can this day get any better*? she thought.

"Good morning, Miss Garrison. I hope your day is going well."

"Why, yes, it is, Mr. Clay. And how about yours?"

"Well, you really don't want to hear the gory details of a vet's early morning call to treat a horse's impaction colic. But, pleased to report, treatment was productive."

"Oh … well … perhaps the details would be less unpleasant than what the mind imagines."

He laughed: "Just status quo in the life of a vet."

"I'll have to start making notes of my own disgusting procedures, so we can trade war stories."

"Ha, I know mine will be bigger, if not better—of course, depending on your definition of 'better.'"

"I don't know about that—I've had a couple of bariatric patients over the years that were particularly challenging."

"Uh, okay, enough shop talk. We'll save it for

another time … when we run out of other things to say."

"Not the stuff of relationship building, I guess," she agreed.

"Not the kind of relationship I had in mind." Jemma heard horses snorting in the background. "On a more positive note, I'll be in Ranchester Friday and Saturday and thought we might get together for dinner Friday evening. Would you be free?"

"I'll have to check my heavy appointment calendar and see." Teasing, she paused for a moment. "Hmm … yes."

"Great, what time? I can pick you up at Virgil's or meet you some place."

"I'm working the early shift in ER, so I'll have plenty of time to get home and get cleaned up. Any time you're finished that's best for you."

"Well, I'll need to clean up and change too—who knows where my hands and feet will have been that day …"

"Enough," declared Jemma, laughing.

"I can pick you up at the house at six … okay?"

"Sounds good."

"And nothing fancy. Just throw on some jeans, and put those big feet in your cowboy boots," he ordered.

"Sounds even better. See you then."

Jemma felt her world was coming together in a good place—the baby, the potential relationship with Seth, her work, and now her own home. Only a few months ago, she had felt her life dark and disorganized, and now … well, each "today" was full of joy and eager anticipation of tomorrow.

She had just put the keys in the ignition when the phone rang again. Answering, she heard the words, "Jemma, this is Keeton Fox. I'm in town and thought we might get together for lunch or dinner."

*Be assertive*, she told herself. "Mr. Fox, I'm afraid that won't be possible. I have few openings in my schedule these days. And any free time I'm saving for an important project I have underway."

"I understand," he replied, "But I promise to check with you occasionally to see if I can fill one of those rare openings. I must tell you, your artistic perception and your words of understanding of my work seem to be playing on a loop in my brain."

She smiled at his clever line, and responded, "That must be terribly annoying. Well, I won't be available anytime soon. I am so grateful for all you have done, and I wish you only the best … and much success … in all your endeavors." She tapped the red phone icon on her phone.

## Chapter 18

Friday arrived, and Jemma and Tina, her coworker, were staying busy folding clean sheets and towels to store near the beds in the ER unit. Tina observed: "We're either all off or all on down here. Either the day goes by at slug speed, or we're going too fast to eat or get a bathroom break. Once I realized I was doing both at the same time— just happened to have some crackers in my pocket."

Jemma cackled at the picture Tina suggested. She enjoyed Tina's sense of humor and realized she likely needed it as a full-time ER nurse. Like Tina said, the work could be slow and boring or frantic with activity to treat a serious trauma emergency.

"You have anything interesting coming up this weekend? Any man in your life?" Tina asked.

"As a matter of fact, I have a dinner date this evening," Jemma responded with satisfaction.

"Oh … serious?"

"Could be."

"Do I know him? Have you managed to find some handsome, available doctor around here? If so, I'd like to know where he's been hiding."

"No … well, he is a doctor of sorts—a vet."

"Tall, dark, and handsome?" Tina inquired.

Jemma answered, "No, very tall, blond, and boyishly good-looking—big dimples and curly hair."

"Well, you two are probably a striking couple— tall, blond, beautiful." She added, "I like to think my boyfriend and I are beautiful, even if we are short, dark, and dumpy."

Jemma's laughter turned to attention at the sound

of the EMT alert phone. Tina hurried to take the call. She made notes on the nearby clipboard, as they both heard the speaker's voice: "EMT Jackson, County Ambulance. Transporting unconscious patient suffering head trauma, scalp laceration, and possibly multiple broken ribs. Vital signs currently stable. Request neurologist on call at arrival. ETA ten minutes."

"We're on," Tina announced, hanging up the phone. "Prepare cubicle one, and I'll get the neurologist on duty down here."

Jemma moved with the efficiency of nursing skill, honed by years of training and experience. She raised the head of the bed and covered it with fresh sheets. She laid out the materials necessary to clean the head wound, deal with bleeding, and bandage against infection. She moved the IV drip pole close to the bed in preparation for administering fluids and medication.

"Nurse … Garrison," the doctor announced, as he came into the cubicle and noted her name tag, "I'm Dr. Hassam, the neurologist on call. Go ahead and get a bag of Ringer Lactate ready and have fosphenytoin on standby in case of seizure. We can't risk that with broken ribs that could puncture a lung."

"Yes, Dr. Hassam, right away." With the habit of controlled speed, Jemma complied, then heard the shriek of the ambulance siren pulling into the ER dock. Tina and Dr. Hassam raced to meet the stretcher as Jemma prepared an immediate IV.

Moving the stretcher next to the bed, one of the EMTs said, "Okay, this guy's big. Let's get it right the first time. One, two, three …" They carefully transferred the patient to the gurney, and Jemma turned to find and clean a venous entry and insert the IV catheter. Beneath a tangle of blood-matted hair, she saw Seth's face, his expression still, his form unmoving. She felt life and energy draining from her body, as Tina called, "Jemma!" and she moved with renewed energy, speed, and a determination to do whatever she could to help him. Keeping alive and helping him heal now had become the most important project in her life.

When Seth was moved to radiology for a CT scan, Tina logged notes in the computer and Jemma straightened the cubicle in preparation for the aides who would clean and disinfect. Calling across the floor, Tina observed, "I thought you were going to freeze on me for a moment there. I know you've seen worse than that."

Disposing needles in the hazardous waste container and the soiled sheets in the laundry hamper, Jemma removed her gloves and tossed them in the waste can before dispensing sanitizer into her hands. "Yes, but never on someone that close to me."

Tina swung around in her chair toward Jemma. "You mean you know him?"

Jemma joined Tina at the desk behind the counter and sat heavily in a neighboring seat. "Let's just say, I won't be having that dinner date this evening."

"Oh, Jemma, I'm so sorry. But you know he's received good care—Jackson's one of the best EMTs around, and Dr. Hassam is on top of the situation. The scan should clarify his condition, but you know patients can present with some ugly injuries and be up and about in a day or two like nothing ever happened."

"I know. It was just the shock of seeing him like that. Seth has no family—he's like a son to my Uncle Virgil." Jemma sat up and reminded herself: "I need to call him and let him know what's happened ... but I'll wait for a report on his condition."

Tina called the ICU desk and asked to be notified when they had information on Seth Clay. "His immediate family is waiting for news," she said, nodding at Jemma to assert the validity of her statement. For over an hour, Jemma busied herself with mundane duties while she waited for the results. When the phone rang, Tina answered: "ER Nurse Edwards. Yes, Seth Clay." Jemma locked eyes with Tina, who listened intently for a time, then said: "Okay. ICU Bed 3? Yes, the notes are in the computer. … We'll bring the bag with his belongings up to the desk. Thanks."

Tina ended the call and took a deep breath. "The CT showed a subdural hematoma in the frontal lobe. At this point, they don't think they'll have to decompress. He also has two fractured ribs and one broken one in the middle rib cage that is a concern, though it hasn't punctured the lung. He'll be in ICU at least a day or two, then moved to a room. He likely won't be in hospital long, but it will take some weeks for the broken rib to mend."

The report was not the best, but Jemma knew it could have been much worse. "I'm going to take a break and call Uncle Virgil," she informed Tina. "Can I get you anything?"

"No, I'm fine. Take your time. We're back in 'calm before the storm' mode again. I'll page you if you're needed."

The nurses' lounge was empty. Jemma wanted no food but opted for a cup of strong coffee with cream and sugar, before settling into an armchair to call her uncle. When he answered, she said, "Uncle Virgil, I'm on a break, but I need to let you know Seth has been injured and is going to be admitted." She waited for his response, questioning her about the accident. "I overheard the EMTs say he was treating a horse that was supposedly sedated, but the horse kicked him in the head and Seth fell against something that cracked two ribs and broke a third." She allowed Virgil to comment and then continued: "No, he doesn't require surgery at this point, but he'll be in ICU until he's awake. They'll observe him a day or two, then move him to a room. … Yes, he'll be in a lot of pain and need some strong meds—and about six weeks to heal." She responded to Virgil, "No, there's no need to come to the hospital now, not until he's conscious and responsive—maybe later today. I'll keep you posted. You and Catherine just stay busy—and pray. … Yes, love you too."

It was not even noon yet, and Jemma felt drained and noticed the shaking of the cup in her hand. *Adrenalin's an interesting thing*, she thought. It seemed, at least in her own physical make-up, when it kicked in, she became a fine-tuned machine functioning at optimum efficiency—detailed factual recall, sharpened focus, high-performance. Then, like now, when the adrenalin surge subsided, she was a weak, shaky creature—*I might struggle to remember my own name*. She shook her head, took a deep breath, and bowed her head in her own silent prayer. Then, she relaxed against the comfort of the cushioned chair back. She would do what she could to care for Seth, even after his discharge, knowing Virgil and Catherine would be ready to help, *We're family*, she reminded herself. *Family takes care of its own.*

# Chapter 19

Jemma parked the Subaru, engine running and heater warming, at the discharge door and waited while Uncle Virgil got out to meet Seth and the aide pushing his wheelchair. Jemma knew today was the beginning of a lengthy and uncomfortable recuperation, but Dr. Hassam's assurance that healing would come with time seemed a declaration of answered prayer.

Virgil and the aide removed a light blanket from Seth's legs, helped him to his feet, lowered him gingerly into the passenger's seat that was pushed as far back as it would go, and covered him. The grimace on Seth's face revealed the movements were painful, but he was cautious about holding his side or putting any pressure on his chest with the seatbelt. The nurse handed Jemma medicines and hospital-furnished supplies in a paper bag. A large plastic one with the clothing and personal items he had at admission she handed to Virgil, who settled it next to him on the floorboard, as he stretched his long frame across the back seat. When settled, Seth said, "Well, this is a fine mess I've gotten us into. … Remember Laurel and Hardy, Mr. Virgil?" His voice was weak and labored.

"They were almost before *my* time, Seth. How do you know about Laurel and Hardy?"

"I've got the complete collection of their movies on DVD at my apartment. I'll bring them down and we can watch sometime," he finished breathlessly.

Jemma interjected, "Seth, you don't have to make conversation. You can do your deep breathing without straining to talk."

"Mr. Virgil, you were supposed to come with sweet

Nurse Garrison, not Nurse Ratched." Concentrating on driving carefully, Jemma was glad she couldn't see his dimpled smile and lose her disciplined composure.

"She may cut back on your pain meds if you don't follow Nurse Ratched's—that is, Nurse Garrison's instructions," Virgil teased. "When we get home, you may find Nurse Catherine even more Ratchedy than Nurse Jemma."

There was silence in the car, then Seth spoke up to complain: "I really don't like moving in with you and Catherine for six weeks. You guys are newlyweds—you need your space and your privacy."

"You never mind about that," Virgil ordered. "Catherine is buzzing around, all excited—'Like having one of my boys back home,' she said. Of course, you'll likely have to go on a diet of cabbage soup when your time's up and she's finished fattening you with all her good cooking … and my cinnamon rolls."

"If it weren't for the remodeling going on at Uncle Virgil's house, you could stay downstairs there," Jemma stated. "But I'll be at work most days, and Uncle Virgil and Catherine will be around if you need them. I'll come over in the evenings to check on you—be your unofficial home health nurse."

"The remodeling of *your* home," Virgil corrected her. "That's true, but also, 'at home' visits might be awkward, explaining to the social worker why you have a young single man held captive in the master bedroom."

Seth coughed and blurted, "Don't make me laugh, Mr. Virgil."

Virgil leaned over the center console to speak: "Seth, you're a grown man now—we're both adults. Despite the forty plus years I have on you, please, don't call me 'Mr. Virgil' anymore. Okay? I'm just Virgil."

"Yes, sir" Seth responded. "Will do … or will not do … whatever … Uncle Virgil."

Jemma caught Virgil's attention in the rearview mirror and mouthed, "Brain trauma."

Arriving at the house, Jemma took a wheelchair from the hatchback, opened it, and rolled it to the passenger's side where Virgil was beginning to extricate Seth. "We'll do this as easily and painlessly as we can," Virgil told him, as he helped Seth turn to move his legs out of the car.

Catherine met them at the kitchen entrance near the driveway, where Virgil had installed a short ramp over the two steps leading into the house. Catherine called, "Seth, it's so good to see you out of that hospital bed."

"Thanks, ma'am. It's good to feel the fresh air."

Taking Seth's billfold, watch, and keys from his bag of personal items, Jemma followed them through the kitchen and into a downstairs bedroom Catherine had arranged for his stay. "I hope you'll be comfortable here." She pointed out "a half-bath right there with clean towels on the shelf and toiletries in the cabinet and shower." A TV and DVD player were stationed on the chest of drawers across from the bed that appeared to be elevated and king-size. Catherine continued: "Virgil laid out some pajamas and a robe and house shoes for you. You're almost the same size, so I think they'll do."

Seth seemed to choke on tears as he responded, "Mrs. Catherine, Mr. Virgil, you are too good to me. I've got stuff at my apartment, but I don't know when I can get it."

"You never mind about that," Virgil said. "Jemma's off tomorrow, and we'll drive up to Hardin and get what you need."

Jemma informed him: "I put your watch and

billfold there on the nightstand, and I have your keys, if you can show us which one is to your apartment. We'll pick up clothes and anything else you want while you're here. Just tell Uncle Virgil what and where to find it."

Catherine threw back the spread and folded it neatly on the bench at the foot of the bed. "Seth, you ought to rest now," she declared, turning down the blanket and sheet and fluffing a pillow to put in front of another to raise Seth's head. "You let me know if you're comfortable—warm enough … too warm, too cool. Virgil, why don't you help Seth get cleaned up and changed—he'll feel better. Jemma can go over his medication schedule with me."

Jemma noted Seth was quiet, likely tired after the travel. She figured the pain medication should last through his clean up and change, then another dose would help him get some needed rest. Kneeling in front of the wheelchair to face Seth, Jemma said, "Seth, I'm going over to *my* house to see the workmen before they leave. I'll be back and bring something special for dinner and eat with you."

Seth looked at her, placed his hand on hers, and said quietly, "Thank you."

As the women entered the kitchen, Catherine said, "Jemma, you don't have to bring him food. You know we have plenty—I always fix supper for Virgil."

"I know, Catherine, but I thought I'd get some food from the Indian restaurant where we ate after your reception. I'm curious if he'll remember. I want to see his reaction. … And I want him to know I'm going to be close by—I'm not going to bail on him. I'll bring enough for all of us, and you won't have to fix supper this evening."

"Thanks, but I'm afraid, at this age, Virgil and I must be less adventurous with our food. I'll set up a card table in

Seth's room, and you two can eat dinner in there." Catherine provided a tray for the medicines, and Jemma began retrieving bottles from the sack and organizing them. Catherine watched as Jemma read labels and made a simple chart of times and dosages. "You've become quite taken with Mr. Seth Clay, haven't you?" she observed.

Jemma glanced at her and smiled, "I guess you could say that."

"Well, that's nice. I happen to know Virgil has thought, for quite a while, that you and Seth would be a great match—if Seth could get past losing Rachel and you could get past being hurt by 'that dirty no-good cretin,' I think Virgil called him."

"Well, Uncle Virgil's come up with another adept assessment—previously, it was 'charlatan and scoundrel.' One might think he'd even met the man."

Catherine laughed, then looked at her watch. "You'd better get going if you're going to see the workmen before they leave for the day."

"Yes, better run. Here you go." Jemma handed the tray to Catherine. "I think this is self-explanatory. Hopefully, we'll see continual improvement over the next few weeks—the blood gradually will reabsorb. But we'll need to keep a watch for any unusual behavior or new symptoms." Jemma opened the kitchen door to leave. "By the way, I have the bag with the clothes he was wearing when the EMTs brought him—I'll launder those and bring them when I come back."

"Okay, dear. Just a moment." Catherine came to the door to give Jemma a hug and ask, "Have I told you how proud I am to be your aunt—great aunt, that is?"

"No, but not any prouder than I am to be your great-niece. I'm so happy Uncle Virgil can spend the rest of his life with you—with his second-best girl across the street," she grinned.

# Chapter 20

Jemma entered the bedroom to find Seth sitting in a chair at the card table Catherine had arranged with a tablecloth and dinnerware, a decanter of cold water, even a small vase with two roses, the last of her seasonal flowering. "You must be hungry—you're already seated and ready for food," she observed.

"Catherine said you called to say you were on your way. I'm not sure if I'm hungry or just looking forward to Indian food. I assume it's from Mumbai—that was delicious when we ate there after the wedding."

With a sigh of satisfaction at his remembrance, Jemma said, "Yes, it was." Arranging containers on the table, she declared: "I chose my favorites—beef curry, spinach paneer, vegetable fritters, rice, naan, and kheer for dessert. I pick up the food, I pick out the food!"

"Wow, fine by me. It smells wonderful." Seth extended his hand to take hers and gave thanks for the food, followed by, "You didn't have to do this."

"I know," she teased. "You gave me a reason to indulge again."

Tasting some morsels she served him, he declared: "Well, it's as good as it was last time—so is the company," he grinned, before his expression changed to curiosity. "How are the renovations coming along at Virgil's— excuse me at *your* house?"

"The workmen are moving fast, seems to me. Of course, I don't know about such things, but I wouldn't be surprised if Uncle Virgil really lit a fire under them to get the project finished. I think the home study will go well when they see the accommodations we'll have for Melissa.

The bathroom renovation will be the most time-consuming, I think. Oh, and the master carpenter has come to take measurements for the gates on the stairs, at the top and the bottom."

"When will the first home visit be?" he asked.

"I'm not sure—likely soon, in the middle of all the disruption of building. But at least the social worker will be able to report what we're doing—that we're investing time and money in making the house safe and suitable for a child."

They ate their food in silence for a few minutes, before Seth said, "I was blessed to have grandparents who took me in when my parents died. But, for children like Melissa, who have no family, to have a home like the one you will provide—well, it's just great."

Seth took another piece of the bread Jemma offered, as she asked, "I don't want to intrude, but what happened to your parents? Uncle Virgil's never told me about them."

"He never knew them, as far as I know," he replied. "I was very young when they died in an automobile accident near Ranchester. I came to live with Grandma and Grandpa Clay here in Sheridan ... until Rachel and I married ... right out of high school. Well, Grandpa had died by that time, so Rachel and I lived with Grandma— for the sake of finances, but also to help with her care. Grandma didn't live much longer after Grandpa died—she had broken heart syndrome, I think."

"That's an interesting phenomenon, isn't it?" Jemma stated. "'Stress-induced cardiomyopathy,' physicians say, but truly, just inability to go on without the half that made you whole."

"Exactly." Pausing, Seth continued, "I felt it, I know, when Rachel and the baby died. ... But I was young, strong … couldn't give up on life yet, though I couldn't imagine life without them. I was what … twenty? I did 'lose myself' for a while—went up into the mountains … even thought … hoped … I might fall off a cliff or something. I knew it would be wrong intentionally to do away with myself, but I wanted to give providence … or mere chance, every opportunity."

"I'm glad you came back to your senses and are here now," Jemma said softly, then laughed, "having been kicked nearly senseless by an unhappy horse."

"And I had that guy sedated," he informed her, shaking his head. "This vet business is risky. You'd be surprised how many vets are injured in a year—often seriously."

"Well, your situation could be far worse than just six weeks of recuperation," she reminded him.

"Yes. I know one vet with a similar injury who'll never be the same. Most of us carry disability insurance—we know the odds are against us." Seth took a spoonful of kheer from the container and said, "Um, that's good, but you eat the rest. I'm full to the eyeballs."

Giggling, Jemma took the container and responded, "I can do that."

"Good. You could use a few extra pounds—your feet will look smaller," he teased.

"Well, good to see you're back to your meanie old self," she retorted, grinning. "Unfortunately, some things can't be knocked out."

Seth put his head in his hand, breaking their mutual gaze.

Jemma looked at her watch and stood, as she stated, "It's time for your meds. I'll be back."

Seth took the pills she brought, and she asked,

"How about you lie down now?"

"In a few minutes … when I get sleepy. … I don't like taking painkillers and steroids, but these headaches are intense."

"Sadly, they're to be expected but should pass in time." Jemma watched him closely for any further signs of distress. "Have you noticed any other symptoms—visual … auditory …"

"No, no, nothing … just the occasional headache. I want to get back to normal ... back to being the caretaker, not the patient."

"Well, I'm sure your patients are missing you, especially that one that nearly knocked your brains out," she remarked.

"I've been doing some thinking about …" His thought trailed away as he said, "I'm sorry, Jemma. I think I do need to lie down now. I'm sorry to leave you with this clean up."

"Don't be silly. I'll take care of it. Do you need the walker?"

"No, I'm okay. I can make it," he affirmed, as he leaned on the table to stand.

"Before I clean the table, I'm going to get my stethoscope and cuff and check your vitals." She watched and waited for him to return safely to the bed. *I love him*, she thought, surprised only by the clarity and conviction of the awareness. She was thankful he was with Uncle Virgil and Catherine, only a short walk across the street from Garrison House. They would care for the man she loved, until, if he would allow it, she could devote the rest of her life to caring for him herself.

# Chapter 21

Part of Jemma wanted Uncle Virgil to know the extent of her feelings for Seth. But during the eighty plus miles to Hardin, she had only managed to make small talk and observations on the scenery through which they traveled. "We can put the back seat down if we need the space," Jemma said, as she and Virgil pulled the SUV into the parking space in front of Seth's apartment.

"No need, dear, since we have the clothes bar up. He said his suitcase in the closet should hold everything else. There's room in his briefcase for important papers." Taking a folded paper from the pocket of his suede vest and handing it to Jemma, Virgil said, "This is the list of what he wants."

Virgil opened the door to a tidy efficiency apartment, with simple furnishings and few personal touches, yet felt comfortable and warm. An armchair and foot stool sat beside a bookcase with three shelves holding the ample collection Seth had mentioned that day at the bookstore. The regional history books did far outnumber the medical texts on the bottom shelf. At the left of the chair, an end table held a reading lamp, a note pad and pen, and a photograph Jemma assumed was of Seth and Rachel on their wedding day. Jemma picked up the picture for a closer look and remarked, "Rachel was beautiful … very dark—was she … "

"She was half Crow." Virgil moved to look over Jemma's shoulder. "Yes, she was a pretty girl—as sweet and soft-spoken as she was attractive. The prejudice that might have been an issue in high school was preempted by her kind and gentle nature."

Jemma paused in thought. "Uncle Virgil, does 'bi-racial' in Wyoming mean Native American and White?"

"Why, yes, usually. The percentage of population that is African-American is very low, so here one would assume 'bi-racial' would be Native American and White."

"The nurse at the hospital said Melissa's birthmother declared she was Hispanic, but the nurse said she surely looks bi-racial. I guess the appearances would be similar, whether Hispanic or biracial."

"Yes. You know … just a thought … the mother may have declared herself Hispanic and left the baby to avoid declaring her true identity and ethnicity. I think, according to law, a baby born to a Native American or biracial mother would be a ward of the tribe, not of the State. … But," Virgil declared, "Melissa is not going to be half anything. She is going to be one hundred percent Garrison and one hundred percent loved." Taking the photograph from her, Virgil set it back on the table and said, "I think you and Melissa are going to be the long-needed patches to fix the holes in Seth's heart."

"You really think so, Uncle Virgil?" Jemma asked.

"No doubt about it, dear," he answered. "He loves you. I know." Putting his arm around her shoulders, he added, "And I know you love him. I knew you would … when you stopped beating yourself up for falling for that pathetic excuse of a man … what's his name … Cootie?"

"Cory," she laughed, "but he was pretty lousy." Unfolding the list Virgil had made, Jemma said, "I'll start on the clothes, if you want to get his briefcase and papers. I'll get the box in the car for his books, for when he feels like reading again."

Returning with the container, Jemma began checking the titles on the bookshelf.

"You can leave the medical books for now," Virgil

stated.

"Yes, I'm sure it will be a while before he's ready to deal with another ornery horse," she agreed.

"I'm sure about that, but—I may be speaking out of turn—Seth has been talking about giving up his vet work. It's too risky for a fellow who now looks forward to a long, settled future, I imagine," he grinned with a wink to Jemma.

"He would do that?" she asked.

"Well, I knew he would at some point. When I told you I had the Emporium's future in good hands, I meant Seth's. He's agreed to my turning the reins over to him when I'm gone. Now that Catherine and I are married, I want to do that sooner rather than later. I want to be free to travel with my bride … to spend time with Melissa … just to be free from the day-to-day oversight of the business. With this accident and his assessing the vet business, I think Seth would be agreeable to taking over when he's fully recuperated."

"You think he would be content with less adventurous work?" she smiled.

"Oh, no doubt. He seemed to really enjoy his duties at the Emporium all those years ago—took a real interest in whatever job I gave him. And, when he comes into Sheridan these days, I think he comes by to check on his future enterprise as much as to visit with me." Virgil moved toward the bedroom nook and opened the door to the clothes closet. "There's not much in here. I'll just load up the stuff from these overhead baskets into the suitcase and put the hanging things on the bar."

Jemma managed to get most of the non-medical books in the box, then placed the picture of Seth and Rachel on the top before folding the lid. She felt the future belonged to her and Seth, but she knew Rachel and the baby would always be tucked away in the treasure room of Seth's memories, hopefully now, within walls which would shield from the pain of remembering.

# Chapter 22

"So, you are the only one living in this house?" Stella Abrams asked, as she sat on the loveseat before the fireplace and made notes in her portfolio.

"Yes," answered Jemma. "The house is now solely mine. My uncle married several weeks ago. He has moved into his wife's home and has deeded the house to me. He and Catherine will be regular visitors and occasional babysitters, if that is a consideration in your report."

"I may check in with them and ask a few questions, just to cover the bases. I don't believe there will be any problem at all. As I told you previously, Mr. Garrison is well-known and respected around town for his benevolence and involvement—a 'pillar of the community,' I guess you'd say."

"Ms. Abrams ..." Jemma began.

"Please, call me Stella," she corrected her. And, really, I'm *Mrs.* Abrams. My husband is an estate attorney. Your uncle is one of his clients."

"Oh, really? Well, okay ... Stella," Jemma responded with a smile. Then, with furrowed brow, she continued: "How is the baby? Is she eating well, growing ... content? I'm praying we can move the placement along as quickly as possible. I know the longer the delay, the more challenging the process of attachment."

"You are correct about that. But the baby is a beautiful little butterball, still with a headful of dark hair. She's already smiling and cooing. The foster parents have two children of their own, so Melissa never lacks for attention. As far as the process is concerned, I'm trying to get the visits and reports done within six to eight weeks, so legal custody placement should be shortly thereafter. The final adoption decree may take several months longer, depending on the court's schedule. The main thing is getting little Jane—or Melissa, in your arms," she smiled, "so you can begin those late-night feedings. Better get all the sleep you can while you can," Stella advised with a smile. Looking down at her notebook, Mrs. Abrams continued her questioning: "And is there a husband, boyfriend, significant other who will be in the picture?"

Jemma hesitated. "Well, there is someone very important in my life, though we have made no proclamations or commitments," she grinned.

"Oh, I'm interested—off the record," she laughed. "Anyone I'd know?"

"I don't think so," Jemma replied. "If you visit Uncle Virgil and Catherine, you may run into him. He is recuperating from an accident at their house. He's like a son to my uncle."

"Not Seth Clay?" she asked with surprise.

"Why, yes. So, you know him?"

"Well, mainly by reputation, which, I must say, is laudable. Word gets around in my field, with connections to the hospital, the courts, and families in the community. It was a terrible thing when he lost his young wife and baby. Many who knew grieved for him and were concerned for his well-being, but he proved himself a man of character and strength when he went off to vet school. He does a lot of charity work up around Hardin and Crow Agency. We've even consulted him a couple of times on domestic cases under investigation up there."

Jemma knew Mrs. Abrams was assessing her reaction when she asked, "So, do we have the budding of a relationship underway?"

Considering her response, Jemma stated: "Well,

honestly, speaking only for myself, I hope so—off the record, of course," she reminded Stella.

"Well, I'll keep that in mind," Stella winked. "Now, how about a look around? Mr. Burnham tells me you are doing quite a bit of renovation."

Jemma stood to lead Stella past the stairs to the second floor, as she responded, "Yes, as you see, we have made the stairwell secure with locking gates at the top and bottom. We have covered the electrical outlets and placed child-proof latches on the cabinet doors and refrigerator. We have installed a temperature control on the water heater, upper locks on the exterior doors, and a dust and pollutants filtering system on the furnace."

"Well, it seems you are on top of the safety guidelines and then some," Stella declared.

Jemma laughed, "Well, Uncle Virgil is eager to hold his 'Missy Jane.' He's enlisted his own workmen and likely twisted arms and called in favors to get things done ASAP."

With misty eyes, Stella commented, "This little girl, obviously will want for nothing …"

Jemma interrupted: "She'll never want for love—and love won't spoil her. But she'll learn to be a responsible, contributing part of a family, whose mission is to love and serve others. Catherine and I will have to keep Uncle Virgil under control—he's a threat to be a pushover, a 'Spoiler-in-Chief," she chuckled.

As they entered the newly renovated wing, Jemma directed Stella's attention to the bedroom to the left: "That is my bedroom with a half-bath, study nook, and walk-in closet." As they entered the baby's room next door, Jemma stated, "The nursery is ready to be painted and decorated. I'm leaving that up to Uncle Virgil and Catherine, a talented decorator. She's excited about doing a baby girl's space."

Noting the vanity cabinet with sink on one wall, Stella remarked, "I like that idea for a nursery."

"The changing table with shelves will be incorporated with the vanity as a unit, with supplies conveniently nearby for cleanups and diapering," Jemma replied. She continued to the right end of the hallway. "This is the new enlarged bath. We moved the plumbing and fixtures, so the nursery would be next door to my bedroom. There's a door from my bedroom into the nursery, and the bathroom is accessible from the nursey through the clothing and supplies closet. We installed a separate toilet and hand sink, a shallow tub and shower combination, extended counterspace with double vanity, and ample cabinet space."

"Well, this is most impressive. I look forward to seeing the finished wing in a few weeks. I'll try to finish my interviews and complete my final report; and, if all is ready then, we can see about setting the date to grant legal custody. Then, with no other custody claims, we can move directly toward the declaration of adoption."

"That's so good to hear," Jemma sighed. "I'm ready for this new life of motherhood. I want to be a good mother … a good mother for Melissa."

# Chapter 23

Jemma pulled the collar of the wool sweater up around her neck and adjusted her scarf. The coldest weather would soon arrive, and she prayed Melissa would be settled soon in the love and warmth of her forever home. This would be one of Jemma's few remaining days off without the responsibilities of motherhood, so she was determined, even compelled, to check off the remaining tasks on her list of preparations. Catherine had told her, "Go away. Go shopping. Go eat lunch with Virgil. Just don't come back until I text you." Catherine was putting finishing touches on the nursery, and she wanted everything to be perfect before presenting it to Jemma.

Their church friends, who wanted to assess, in person, the baby's size and unmet needs, were planning a "Welcome Shower" shortly after Melissa's arrival. But Jemma realized all immediate needs should be on-hand and ready to go. The cargo area of the Subaru was full of diapers, cases of formula, and the "ultimate" in highchairs. Surrounding the carrier/car seat, properly affixed in the back seat according to safety instructions, were boxes of canned baby food—rice and oat cereal, apples, pears, sweet potatoes, green beans, and two four-packs of anti-colic baby bottles with cleaning equipment.

Checking her watch, she had time to go by the bookstore to get some books and music CDs, *so important to her intellectual development.* And she'd look for a new local history book Seth had mentioned. Almost back to full health and working part-time in Ethan Banning's office, he was now a boarder at Virgil and Catherine's. When they insisted on his staying until he moved to a new apartment in Sheridan, he refused, unless he paid fair rent. After lunch with Uncle Virgil, she would stop by the pharmacy to pick up additional supplies and meds to have on-hand. *Baby wipes*, she thought. *I need to buy cases of baby wipes!*

Considering her day's shopping history, Jemma knew she would need one of the small carts available at the door of the bookstore. In short order, it held a supply of colorful "Recommended" children's books, *A Guide to Care of Baby and Child*, the history book for Seth, and music CDs for babies—classical music, lullabies, sounds of nature, and music for calming and relaxation. Jemma flipped through a few parenting magazines and returned them to the periodicals rack, negatively critiquing their information on how to delegate the responsibilities of parenting to someone else.

Noting the rear entrance nearby, Jemma thought she would revisit the art gallery, though she risked running into Keeton Fox. It had been months now since their initial meeting and her purchase of "Village at Early Morning"— and his surprising presence at the party. Her last contact with him—the call where she clarified there was "an important project underway" in her life, was now several weeks in the past. Though she felt on guard with the artist himself and had discouraged his attention, she reminded herself he had never been forward, only kind; and his paintings still touched her emotions and stirred her imagination.

Jemma moved along the display wall, where some familiar works remained, but a few had been added since her last visit. She was drawn to one called "Two Worlds"—the portrait of a young woman, she assumed Native American, her elbow resting on the frame of what appeared to be an open truck window. The breeze blew tendrils of black hair around her soft, misty brown eyes. It seemed as if she had turned toward the driver in reaction to some comment or question. But the expression was curious—a slight smile tinged with what? Sadness … disappointment … fear?

"She's a beautiful woman, don't you think?"

Hearing the familiar voice, Jemma sighed and turned to see Keeton Fox approaching to stand next to her. "Oh, hello, *Mr. Fox*. Yes, indeed, she is. Who is she?" Jemma asked.

"Just a girl I knew. It was the last time I saw her, but the memory is etched in my brain."

Jemma was hesitant to continue a conversation, but she was curious. "The painting makes apparent you were very special to each other."

"Again, you are perceptive," he stated. Fox moved to speak directly to Jemma. "Please, call me Keeton. Surely, we can be on a friendly, first name basis."

Jemma tilted her head, briefly considered a response, and answered, "Professionally friendly," she smiled. "A busy registered nurse and the talented artist whose work she appreciates, whether it is painting canvases or cakes." She turned again to study the painting.

He seemed to read her mind when he stated, nodding toward the canvas: "You are wondering what happened to our relationship. As the title plate indicates— 'Two Worlds' with separate orbits." Looking into the cart and changing the subject, Fox picked up the baby care manual and asked, "Interesting. Is there any news you might share with your friendly professional?"

Jemma took the book from his hand and returned it to the cart, "Well, it soon will be common knowledge that I am in the process of adopting a baby girl—a lovely little Hispanic girl with a head full of black wavy hair. My uncle has named her Melissa. The mother gave away her rights to the child after birth, and the baby was in the nursery—a "Baby Jane" awaiting foster placement, when I took the nursing job. From the first time I held her, I knew we needed each other." Jemma noticed the intensity of Keeton's interest, the softening of his demeanor as he heard her words. "She's with foster parents now, but I'll have legal custody in a few weeks."

Fox hesitated, studying her face, and digesting the information. Then, taking her hand and holding it between his, he replied: "How wonderful! What a fortunate child. I know you will be the best of mothers and fill her life with beauty."

"Thank you, Keeton," she said, withdrawing her hand. "I appreciate your kind words."

He continued: "Jemma, please let me give you a gift in celebration of the occasion."

"Oh, Keeton, that's not necessary. The baby will have more than enough of everything."

"I'm sure. But let me give *you* something in celebration of your motherhood. I insist." He lifted the "Two Worlds" painting from its hanger and said, "I want this in your home. It will mean so much to me to know it is there, in *one world* of love and joy and acceptance." There seemed to be a tremor in his voice, as he said, "I need this as much as you need Melissa."

Jemma felt tears welling in her eyes, as she responded, "Well, Keeton, after those words, how can I refuse your generosity? Thank you … sincerely."

"I'll have Sharon wrap it and hold it until you can pick it up." Leaning toward her, he gave her a kiss on the cheek and said: "Part of an old prayer says, 'May you face the winds and walk the good road to the day of quiet.' In other words, I wish you and Melissa the best of everything always."

Jemma smiled and thought as he moved away: *Maybe Fox's reputation is not entirely fair. I think we could be real friends.*

Jemma arranged to pick up the painting after lunch, loaded her purchases in the car, and walked to the Emporium, where the doorbell chimed as she entered, and Connie greeted her warmly: "Good afternoon, Jemma! How's the baby prep coming along?"

"Fine, I think. Maybe you can go over my list with me sometime and see if I've forgotten anything."

"Babies, to be so little, seem to need a ton of stuff," she declared, "especially first babies. A mother wants everything to be new, untouched, hygienically pure ... I remember. When number four comes along, you rub the binky on your shirt to get rid of a dust bunny and poke it back in the kid's mouth."

Jemma laughed as she continued to Virgil's office. "Remind me to put binkies on the list," she called. She knocked before opening the door to reveal Seth, sitting in Virgil's chair, and her uncle, sitting in one of the guest seats. "What's going on? Seth, what are you doing here ... there?" she said, gesturing to the executive chair behind the desk.

"Jemma, my dear, take a seat. We'll bring you up to speed on what's transpired."

Jemma sat in the chair next to Virgil, as he continued: "Jemma, as of today, I am resigning and turning Garrison's Emporium over to one of the best employees I've ever had the privilege to work for me—Seth Clay." He laughed at the surprise on Jemma's face. "I'm going to enjoy my remaining years with my lovely bride and my great-great-grandniece."

"But, Seth, what about your vet work?" she asked.

"That horse knocked some sense into me. That's as close as I care to come to being done in by a large animal, and small animal work I'm happy to leave to those with an affinity for all sorts of 'poo' dogs and scratching cats. Virgil's known my interest in the Emporium since I was in high school and has encouraged me over the years to think about taking over for him. All it took for me to 'see the light' was to have a horse kick my lights out," he laughed.

"Wow, this has been a day full of surprises!" Jemma observed.

"Well, fill us in," Virgil directed. "The day is only half gone!"

Jemma related her encounter with Keeton Fox and his gift of the painting.

"Is he wooing you with watercolors?" Seth asked with a cynical grin.

"No, I don't think so," she defended. "He seemed to be genuinely interested and sincere, almost emotional, when I told him about the baby. And I made it clear he and I are only friendly professionals. Changing the subject, are you two ready for a celebratory lunch? I'm starving."

"I'm afraid I have to beg off," Virgil replied. "Catherine needs me—and my height, to help with finishing touches on the nursery." With a grin, he teased, "I know you'll miss my company, but I've persuaded Seth here to take you to lunch. He didn't seem to mind … hope you don't."

"I think I can handle an hour or so with him—if the food's good."

Seth unfolded his long form, now seemingly as tall and strong as ever. "How about some curry and naan?"

"Can't think of anything I'd like better."

"Good, and then I thought we'd go stroll through the park. It'll be a great place to take Melissa in the spring. And, full disclosure, Catherine told me to keep you occupied a couple of hours after Virgil has arrived home and they've finished the nursery."

"Then," Jemma declared, "you can help me unload the car and fill the closet and cabinets with a ton of supplies for one small sixteen-pound baby."

Virgil interjected, "Enjoy your lunch. We'll meet up at the house." Turning at the door, he asked, "Jemma, you want me to take your car home for safe-keeping and let Seth bring you later?"

"That would be great, Uncle Virgil. Here are my keys. I'm in front of the gallery. Do you mind picking up the painting on your way?"

"Will do," he agreed waving over his shoulder as he left.

"Thanks," she called after him. "We'll see you at home for the unveiling of the nursery."

## Chapter 24

Few people were scattered around the Mumbai during the late lunch hour, and the host led Seth and Jemma to a secluded booth in the back corner of the dimly-lit restaurant, red leather seating and gold embellishments adding elements of celebration to the ebony finished woodwork and furniture. "Isn't this where we sat when we ate after the wedding?" Jemma asked.

Seth perused their surroundings, harmonious Indian pop love songs softly playing .in the background. "I think it may be," adding with a dimpled grin, "I was so taken with the company, I didn't really notice."

"The company was *almost* as good as the food," Jemma teased. "I remember I had only toast and coffee that morning and was so busy with wedding prep I hadn't eaten. I was starved."   "You chowed down pretty good," he laughed.

"Well, just get ready for an instant replay," she declared.

The waiter returned shortly after taking their order with bowls of curry, vegetables, rice, and a plate heaped with naan, fresh from the tandoor oven.

"That was so good," Jemma declared, leaning against the back of the cushioned seat. "Nothing tastes better than Indian food, especially when one is ravenous."

"I'm glad we have that in common," he laughed. "I used to be a simple, boring 'meat and potatoes guy.' Now I've added … literally, some spice to my life. How about some kheer and cheese balls?"

"Umm … I might have just a little bit more room,"

Jemma answered. "But we'll have to walk the entire length of the park and back."

"We can do that," he laughed.

As they walked to Seth's truck, he wrapped his arm around her shoulders and pulled her close. "You mind? he asked.

"Not at all. Makes me feel small and protected—that's nice."

They walked in silence for several seconds before Seth continued: "I would like to make you feel small and protected for as long as you would allow—how about the rest of your life?"

Speechless, Jemma looked up at Seth, then stammered, "What?"

Jemma noted Seth's face was becoming flushed as he responded, "I guess that's an awkward way of asking if you could think of me as a permanent fixture in your life. You don't need to say anything. Just think about it."

She leaned her head against Seth's shoulder and replied softly, "I will."

Jemma was glad she had brought along a sweater—the sun barely warmed the chill in the air as they strolled through the park and stopped at the bison display. The largest of three enormous creatures in their enclosure, the male wallowed in the dirt, then rolled to his feet and stood with a bellowing snort. "Our national mammal—amazing creatures, aren't they?" Seth declared. "Can you imagine the thunderous sound of thousands of them stampeding across the prairie?"

"I read tens of millions of them were slaughtered in the nineteenth century," Jemma added.

"That's right. With a tremendous negative impact

on the native peoples who depended on the bison for food, clothing …" Their conversation was interrupted by the message notification on Jemma's phone."

"Excuse me," she said, retrieving the cell from her pocket. With a smile, she informed him: "That's Catherine. She says, 'Come home posthaste,' with a smiley face."

"Well, we'll revisit these hairy beasts come warmer weather. But now, the unveiling of 'Baby Melissa's Wonder World."

"And then, don't forget, unloading the car and assessing if we have everything we need."

"You know, children for millennia have survived and often thrived without a fraction of what this one little girl will have."

Sheepishly, Jemma admitted, "Yes, I know. … I guess it's as much for me as for Melissa. I'm having such fun getting ready."

"Try to remember the fun," he grinned, "when you're weary to the bone, trying to console a hungry, squalling baby … at three in the morning … before an early shift at the hospital."

Punching his shoulder, she chuckled, "Why don't you add 'while dealing with a head cold' for good measure."

"Yeah, right … that too," he laughed.

# Chapter 25

Jemma and Seth entered the house to find Virgil and Catherine resting at the kitchen table before glasses of tea and her uncle wiping his brow with his handkerchief. Virgil declared: "I'm retired. I don't plan to work this hard again until Melissa and I build her playhouse out near the chestnut tree."

Jemma responded, "Well, I think you should have a good three years to recuperate."

Catherine rose from her seat to speak: "Jemma, why don't you and Seth see the room while we wait here. I want your true assessment, and I don't want our presence to influence you. Be completely objective. We can change anything—or everything, whatever you want, but know that I've done my best to make it my vision of a magical little girl's room. Thank you, Jemma, for letting us have a part and such pleasure in fixing up the nursery."

Jemma moved to hug Catherine. "Thanks for all your effort and for all your love. I know it's a special, beautiful place."

Seth followed Jemma to the hallway of the nursery suite and the creamy white door to the baby's room. Set in pale gold walls, the entrance was flanked by white lanterns providing additional soft light for the hallway and entry. The two center panels of the door displayed decoupaged scenes of woodland settings, creatures, and hobbit houses in muted hues; and the horizontal board by the glass doorknob had sandpaper primary letters declaring the room's occupant, "Melissa"—at a suitable height for a child of nursery school age to trace with her finger. "How lovely, and Catherine knows something about Montessori," Jemma commented to Seth, as she smiled and touched the rough surface of the characters.

Jemma opened the door to a tranquil space of softness and light—sage walls with chair rail and trim painted antique white like the door. A chandelier centering the room was festooned with crystal beading draped around a ring of white ceramic rabbits and candle lights with fabric shades that matched the pastel sage, ivory, and blue striped drapes framing the room's center windows. A light gold area rug with cream border and corners trimmed with sage, blue, and rose floral vines covered much of the polished hardwood floor. Centered between the windows a light honey oak chest of drawers supported a white rabbit lamp. To the right of the windows, a play area contained an assemblage of white wicker children's furniture—a rocker draped with a velvety soft pink throw, a tea table where a baby doll waited to be joined in the opposing chair, and a wagon in which a cuddly fox sat perched and ready for a ride. A beige upholstered rocking armchair trimmed in crisp white cording and a matching storage ottoman sat at the left of the windows with, nearby, a white pole lamp and, matching the finish of the chest, a bookcase, where a collection of Dr. Seuss books and a dark brown Teddy bear waited to greet their child.

On the wall outside Jemma's bedroom, Catherine and Virgil had stationed a masterpiece of elegant nursery cribs—soft honey oak with an arched wallboard, which, Jemma assumed, would become the head of a twin bed when Melissa graduated from nursery bedding. "This is the finest, fanciest baby bed I've ever seen," Seth declared, as he moved his hand along the smooth railing.

"Look at those." Jemma directed his attention to a series of paintings above the bed—a lovely triptych in soft watercolors that displayed young local wildlife creatures—a bear cub, a wolf pup, and a fox kit. "Unless I'm mistaken, Keeton Fox has left his mark again. They are beautiful."

Seth sighed, "I can't even draw a good stick horse. I can't compete with that."

Jemma took his arm and leaned her head against his shoulder. "You don't have to compete with anyone."

On the opposite wall near the storage closet pass-through to the bathroom, a pink cushioned changing table extended from the vanity with sink, the entire unit matching the finish of the other honey oak furniture. Above the table, her aunt and uncle had installed white shelves holding baskets of assorted sizes for cleansing and diapering needs; and above the vanity hung a sizeable oval mirror with a frame carved to form a ribbon tied at the top in a delicate pink and sage bow.

"They have done so much," Jemma announced. "It's all so beautiful ..." Jemma sniffed and wiped a tear from her cheek. Seth drew her into his embrace, with the words, "We all love you and want only the best for you and the baby." Retrieving a tissue from a shelf above the changing table, he said, "Here. Come on—let's check out the bathroom."

Jemma and Seth found useful treasures and practical surprises in every corner of the nursery, storage closet, and adjoining bath, where baby woodland animals frolicked on walls and welcomed a little one to join them in their glade. "Look at this." Jemma's smile glistened with tears as she touched the container between the double sinks and sorted through its contents. "A personalized bamboo box filled with bath toys, tearless shampoo, baby washcloths—oh, and even baby toothpaste and toothbrushes," she exclaimed, holding the package to his view. "If I can find a place for all the stuff in the car—and the things our friends and church members may give us, maybe there'll be enough room left for Melissa."

Catherine and Virgil's questioning expressions greeted Jemma and Seth's return to the kitchen. Jemma gave each of them a hug and kiss on the cheek. "Thank you. I have never seen a room more filled with love and beauty than Melissa's nursery. She will be a most blessed little girl—not only because of the things you have given her, but because of your love and care. As has been so often the case, I can't adequately express my gratitude."

Virgil discreetly rubbed his eyes and cleared his throat, as Catherine replied, "You are so very welcome, Jemma. Thank you for letting us help. We are so excited and can hardly wait to hold her in our arms."

"Well, that shouldn't be much longer. I'll call Stella Abrams and let her know everything is finished and we're ready for the final visit and inspection. Hopefully, it will be very soon." Jemma touched Seth's shoulder and asked, "You ready to help unload the car?"

"Sure," he replied, winking at Catherine and stating, "I just hope these two have left enough storage space for all of it."

"Jemma, just a moment, if you don't mind," Uncle Virgil interjected.

"Sure, Uncle Virgil," she replied, turning to see unusual anxiety in his expression.

"Jemma, Catherine has made me realize I owe you an apology. I jumped right in and asked to call the baby 'Melissa Jane' and never thought to consult you. I had no right to do that—you're her mother. I hope you can forgive me. You name her whatever you like."

"Oh, Uncle Virgil, there's nothing to forgive. It's a beautiful name—and, besides," she smiled, "that's the name now on the legal documentation that's being prepared—'Melissa Jane Garrison.'" Wrapping her arm around Virgil's shoulders, she added, "You are the patriarch of the Garrison family—you have the naming right," she laughed. "But you never told me why that name is so special to you."

"Go ahead, Virgil. Tell her," Catherine directed. Turning to Jemma with a wink, she added, "You see, there was a great love in Virgil's life before me."

"What?' Seth questioned. "You never told me."

Jemma's words overran Seth's: "Uncle Virgil, who was she?"

He cleared his throat again before answering: "She was a pretty, sweet, dark-haired little girl, who was kind and gentle to a lumbering, homely giant of a third-grade boy, too big to fight the smaller boys, but not too big to be hurt by their words. I was hiding and crying behind a tree on the playground one afternoon, and Melissa Jane Hardeman found me there. She said, 'Crying always make me feel better ... unless I get a stuffy nose and headache.' She made me laugh, and we became the best of friends— almost to junior high school."

Jemma asked, "What happened to her?"

"Her father got a job in Illinois, and they moved away. A few years back, out of the blue, I got a letter from her congratulating me on my success in Sheridan and telling me all about her life and children. She said she had never forgotten our friendship and wanted to tell me how precious those memories were. She was terminally ill and, while she had time, she was contacting people who had been important to her. It pleased me to know I was among them ... that she remembered."

"What a lovely story," Jemma observed. "When Melissa is old enough to understand, please tell her how she got her name and why it is special. More than anything, I want her to be a kind and loving person like your first Melissa Jane."

Virgil replied, "With your influence and Catherine's, she's sure to be a beautiful, godly woman, I know." He reached to take Catherine's hand and pressed it to his lips.

# Chapter 26

Stella Abram's parting words had been, "I wish you and little Melissa Jane the best of everything. I'll be in touch with information about the adoption. In the meantime, if you have any questions or needs, just call me." With thanks, Jemma had closed the door behind the one whose kindness and thoughtfulness had been key in opening the portal to Jemma's new, forevermore life. Now a foster mother, Jemma rocked her sleeping child and wrapped around her fingers the baby's dark hair, making ringlets. *I could not love this child more had she come from my own body*, she thought. *I must remind myself that with love comes training and discipline. It will be easy to spoil her—Catherine and Uncle Virgil can do that ... within reason. But I must try to keep her grounded ... to instill in her goodness, benevolence ... faith ... courage.* The seriousness of the responsibility creased Jemma's brow.

The doorbell sounded, and Jemma moved to lay the sleeping baby in her crib, covered her with a receiving blanket, and secured the railing. She moved quietly down the hallway and across the living room to the front door, which she opened to find Keeton Fox offering her an arrangement of pink miniature roses and baby's breath in a crystal bowl. "Keeton," she said in surprise.

"I hope you don't mind," he explained, "but I wanted to bring a little something for you and the baby to celebrate her arrival. I called Virgil to see how custody was progressing, and he told me Melissa had arrived this morning. He and Catherine were shopping for some extra supplies."

"Well, thank you. The flowers are lovely," Jemma

replied, accepting the arrangement. "Yes, it's amazing the necessities for one baby. Would you like to see her? She's asleep, but at least you can take a look at her sweet face."

"If you don't mind. I would like that." He stepped across the threshold to follow Jemma. Entering the nursery, he observed, "Catherine did an outstanding job—a little girl's treasure room."

Jemma placed the flowers on the dresser before leading him to the crib. She added, nodding toward the paintings above the baby bed, "Yes, and a very fine artist helped make it special with his artwork—so distinctively yours."

"I'm glad you are pleased," Fox said. Then he stood for some silent moments, apparently enraptured by the sight of the sleeping baby.

Breaking the stillness, Jemma stated: "She's a lovely child, isn't she?"

"Yes, very," he replied. "And I know she will want for nothing, especially for love." Keeton looked at her with moist eyes and placed his hand over hers on the bed railing. "You are a good woman, Jemma."

"Well, thank you, Keeton," she replied, waiting a moment to remove her hand from under his. "And I hope to be a good mother to Melissa."

Keeton kissed his fingers and reached into the bed to lay them on the baby's forehead, then smoothed curls away from her face, causing her to stir. "Sorry to disturb you, baby girl. Sweet dreams." Turning toward the door, he said, "Thank you, Jemma. I must be on my way. I'd like to visit again some time if you don't mind."

"Just call first, please," Jemma directed, "to make sure we're here and it's convenient." With a "Good day" and a strange sense of relief and some unease about future visits, Jemma closed and locked the front door behind her parting guest.

Before her return to the nursery, the bell again chimed, and she opened the front door to Seth, who removed his cowboy hat and declared, "I've come to call on the popular Miss Melissa Garrison. Is she at home and receiving guests?"

"Hello, Mr. Clay. She most definitely is home. She's actually asleep right now, but she's available for viewing in all her slumberous beauty."

Stepping into the room, Seth said, "I saw Fox pulling out of the drive as I came around the corner. Was he visiting the baby, wooing the mother, or both?"

"We'll assume he was visiting the baby. Wooing the mother is not in the cards. Come on back," she said, waiting while Seth removed his boots and explained, "They can be noisy on this hardwood—don't want to wake her."

"Thanks for thinking. I want to keep the rug clean too," she grinned, "though I know the office is no way as dirty as one of your former barn stalls."

"Nor as smelly," he quipped.

Peering into the crib, Seth said, "She's a beauty. Look at all that hair."

"Yes, and she has deep brown eyes, fringed in thick black lashes—so pretty. ... But I don't want her growing up thinking looks are all that important. I want her to learn to love, to serve ... to be a blessing to all who know her."

"And I know you are just the mother she needs to do that," Seth commented. Turning toward the foot stool, he asked, "Mind if I sit?"

Returning to her seat in the rocker, Jemma

answered, "Please do. She'll be awake in maybe half an hour and ready for some lunch if you can hang around for the feeding. It will be the first time I've fed her, and I'm praying for success."

"I'm sure you'll both do fine." Seth pulled a small decorative box from his jacket pocket and handed it to Jemma. "I got Melissa a little something I hope you'll like."

"Why, thanks, Seth." Jemma opened the box to reveal on a white satin cushion a gold baby bracelet engraved with Melissa's name. "How pretty and sweet! I love it. *She* will love it."

"The jeweler said it's made so that as Missy grows, links can be added to enlarge it. She can even add charms later if she likes."

"That's a great idea. Thank you. It's beautiful. We'll put it on her when she wakes up."

Seth reached into his other pocket, stating, "I got something for her mother, too. You know, her mama's mighty special to me." Jemma was motionless as she heard Seth's words: "Jemma, I don't want to face any tomorrows without you and Missy in my life—I mean, really, truly, permanently in my life." He dropped from the footstool to his knee and opened a black velvet box, revealing a white gold setting of two diamonds in the shape of an infinity symbol—"One diamond for you," he explained, "and the other for Melissa. You come as a set, and I want us to be a family, if you'll have me." Chuckling, he added, "I'm afraid you'll have to speak for Melissa. Will you marry me?"

Jemma only took time for a breath before answering, "Yes, oh, yes, Seth, we will marry you," she laughed, pulling him to herself for a hug and kiss. Their exchange caused Melissa to stir and make a noise.

"Melissa wants to answer for herself—I'm sure that was a 'Yes.'"

## Chapter 27

Catherine had come with a box of fresh cinnamon rolls for the nurses' break room and now stood at the kitchen table, as Jemma collected the day's necessities in her bag and tried to still the anxiety rising within her. "Catherine, here is the schedule of her feedings. She's had her bath and her vitamins. You can dress her in whatever you like when she wakes up. You know where everything is." Jemma scurried across the kitchen and opened the refrigerator door. "The bottles are in here ready for the warmer and over there next to the sink, the rice cereal, fruit, and veggies I set out. I should be home no later than five. If you need me, just text my cell, and … uh …" Jemma stopped to sort her thoughts and next course of action, then continued, "Let me go check on Missy one last time."

Catherine caught Jemma by the shoulders as she passed by the table. "Jemma, everything will be fine. You knew the day would come when you would have to return to work and delegate some mothering responsibility. I've raised two boys and cared for all my grandbabies. Melissa will be fine. Virgil is coming over within the hour, and we'll give reports whenever you call. This first day will be the hardest, but you've got patients who need your focused attention."

"You're right. I'm not that far away if there's a problem." Jemma hugged Catherine and reminded her, "You wanted to watch her a day or two a week. We'll see if you still feel that way at five o'clock."

"Oh, I will. And remember, I come a lot cheaper than that fancy nursery care place. You can put a couple days' fees into Melissa's college fund."

Jemma laughed and said, "I'll be right back."

Encased in her soft, warm rose print sleeper, Melissa lay sleeping soundly in the crib. She had kicked off the receiving blanket but still grasped her favorite giraffe teething toy. Jemma was overwhelmed by love and tenderness for her child—soon to be *their* child, she reminded herself. She was thankful for Seth's obvious growing affection for Melissa, and she often wondered if he sometimes thought of his own child, who had died so tragically after Rachel's passing. Baby Virgil likely had the same dark hair and complexion. *Bi-racial children seem to be particularly attractive people*, she thought, as she leaned into the bed to buss Missy's cheek. *Hispanic, bi-racial ... whatever ...* "Mommy loves you, sweet girl. Be happy with Aunt Catherine and Uncle Virgil," she spoke into the child's dreams.

*Oh, I've got to get my street clothes*, she remembered. *I'll shower and change at the hospital so I can grab Missy first thing when I get home.* She collected her things from the walk-in closet in the adjoining bedroom and noticed on her return to the nursery the painting Keeton had given her, now positioned on the wall behind her reading chair and lamp table. *Such a lovely girl—her eyes so dark and expressive*, though Jemma could not pin down the exact emotion they communicated—*an enigmatic "Mona Lisa" of sorts*, Jemma smiled to herself.

After laying her hand softly on Melissa's chest to confirm the regularity of her breathing, Jemma proceeded to the kitchen. She added the clothing change to the handbag and donned her puffy jacket and the gloves taken from the nearby coat rack. Collecting the bag and cinnamon rolls, she headed toward the kitchen door. She called to her aunt, now washing a few remaining dishes in the sink: "Thanks, Catherine. I hope you have a good day. I'll pray all goes smoothly."

"It will," Catherine assured her. "And, if you don't mind, I'll have some supper ready for us here about six. Maybe we can discuss wedding plans if you and Seth are to that point yet."

"Oh, coming home to some of your good food will be wonderful. We'll have to see how Seth feels about wedding talk. We haven't even discussed when—just soon after the final adoption decree. I'll call you on my first break. I love you, Aunt Cat."

The door closed on Catherine's parting admonition: "Love you too, dear. Drive safely. Snow is predicted this afternoon."

# Chapter 28

Excitement overcame Jemma's exhaustion, as she rounded the corner onto Kirkbride and approached her home and Melissa Jane. Seeing Keeton Fox's green Bronco parked in the driveway behind Virgil's truck, she asked aloud with consternation, "What is he doing here?" Jemma parked in the garage, collected her bag, and pressed the remote to close the overhead door. She exited through the side door onto the newly-covered walkway to the kitchen, where Catherine had filled the room with the delicious smells of marinara and freshly baked bread.

"Hello, dear. How was your day?" Catherine asked, as she continued to stir the sauce pot.

Jemma dropped her bag in a chair, joined Catherine at the stove, and whispered, "It was fine. What is Keeton doing here?"

"He just came by to talk to Virgil and to see Melissa. Why? Is that not all right?" she questioned.

Jemma sighed with resignation. "I just told him to call first—not to drop by without checking to see if it was convenient."

"Well, I'm sure he must have asked Virgil. They seem to have had a pleasant visit. He's been here almost an hour. I'm sure he's leaving soon."

"I hope so. Maybe I can go encourage him along." Jemma halted her movement toward the living room to ask, "He's not expecting to stay for dinner?"

"No, Jemma. Neither Virgil nor I would presume to do that. This is your home ... your dinner." Jemma regretted the slight annoyance she sensed in Catherine's response.

Jemma found Virgil lounging on the love seat and Fox seated in the facing armchair, with Melissa comfortably ensconced in his arms and chewing on her giraffe. "Hello, Jemma, this little one is growing so quickly … and such a lovely child."

"Why, thank you, Keeton," Jemma responded, as she moved to retrieve Melissa, clasped her to her chest, and brushed her face in the child's soft dark curls. "Hey, there, baby girl. Mommy has missed you so much today. I could hardly wait to get home." Turning to her uncle, Jemma asked, "How has your day been, Uncle Virgil?"

"Just the best," he answered. "I have fed and rocked and sung and snuggled all day … with both my girls," he chuckled.

"Have you talked to Seth about discussing wedding plans this evening?" she asked.

"Well, I know he's coming over for supper. Catherine likely knows about the planning business." Jemma noted Virgil squinted a bit as he responded, and she wondered if he understood her purpose for asking … and if Keeton understood it would be appropriate to excuse himself.

"Well, this must be an exciting time for you, Jemma," Keeton stated, as he stood and took his overcoat from the back of the chair. "Motherhood and marriage—not necessarily in the usual order," he laughed. "But a time of happiness and celebration." As he moved toward the front door, Virgil stood to follow him and placed his hand on Fox's retreating shoulder.

"Keeton, thanks for stopping by. Good to talk to you."

"Yes, Virgil. Thanks for your time. And, Jemma, please let me know if there is anything I can do to help with your preparations. Remember, I'm a creative cake decorator."

"Thanks, Keeton. I do remember. I appreciate all your artistic talent—and the beauty it has contributed to our home."

"You are so welcome," he replied as he opened the door and turned to blow a kiss toward Melissa with the words, "Bye, baby girl. See you soon, love."

After Fox's departure, Jemma moved to take his place in the chair and seated Melissa on her knees to sing and play pat-a-cake, bringing her little one to smiles and excited giggles.

Virgil took his place again on the loveseat, then observed, "I have the feeling you weren't pleased to find Keeton here when you got home. I thought you might ask him to stay for dinner."

Jemma continued to clap Missy's hands as she explained: "I hope I didn't come off as rude. He has been very generous. I appreciate that. ... and interested, even concerned about us at times. But, Uncle Virgil, he makes me uncomfortable. I'm sorry if that offends you—I know you are friends."

"Well, I can't say that exactly. I've known of his work and his reputation for years, but I only came to deal with him on a personal basis after you moved here and made his acquaintance. From this man's perspective, I think he's found you an attractive, challenging romantic pursuit. He seems a good man, just kind of slick with his approach."

"Yes, I guess ... that's likely why he makes me uncomfortable." Taking a deep breath, she continued, "Subliminal memories, don't you know," she suggested with a wink.

They heard the movement of the kitchen door and

Seth's voice: "Whew, it's getting cold and windy out there. Snow's a-coming. Boy, I hope that food tastes as good as it smells, Aunt Cat. Where are my girls?"

"In here, Seth," Jemma called.

Seth came to Jemma's chair, gave her a quick kiss, and met Missy's outstretched arms to pick her up and lift her into the air as she squealed with joy. "You are just perfection, Melissa Jane Garrison, and I love, love, love you!"

"How about her mother?" Jemma laughed.

Setting Missy back on Jemma's lap, he kissed her and declared, "And I love, love, love you, too, Miss Garrison."

Virgil interjected, "That reminds me … while I've got you together, I have a proposition."

Seth sat on the footstool next to Jemma and Missy to give Virgil his attention.

Virgil continued: "Since you two will be married and Melissa's adoption will be finalized at some point—and since you're going to be Missy Jane's daddy, Seth, I think it only right and fitting the name on that adoption decree should be 'Melissa Jane Clay.' Don't you agree?"

"Uncle Virgil … why, I did not even think …" Jemma began.

Seth continued, "Virgil, I would be so proud to be her legal, adoptive father—but, you know, she will always be a Garrison, just like Jemma."

Jemma thought for a moment before declaring: "Seth, Uncle Virgil, as her legal custodian, I'm going to ask to have the name on the final decree be changed to 'Melissa Jane Garrison Clay.' That's what I want … okay?"

Virgil raised his glasses and rubbed his eyes. "Whatever you decide, Jemma. That would make me so proud."

"As it would me," Seth agreed. "Melissa Jane Garrison Clay."

They laughed together when Virgil re-adjusted his specs and added, "Until some stinkin' man comes along and marries her."

# Chapter 29

Melissa's cry of hunger awakened Jemma to the coziness of a snowy day in the comfort of her warm home. She relished days like these, when she could free herself of work concerns and responsibilities and focus on time with her daughter.

"Good morning, sweet Missy. How's my beautiful little girl this morning?" Jemma cooed, as she leaned over the fussy baby. Jemma was overjoyed when, at the sound of her voice, Melissa's crying stopped, and the baby smiled and reached for her mother. Jemma lifted Missy, hugged her to her chest, and nuzzled the softness in the crook of her neck. "You are growing so fast. I want to hold you in my arms forever," she declared. Moving to the changing table, Jemma continued: "But, you are a wet goose, my girl. Let's get you changed and dry, and we'll fix us some breakfast."

The kitchen was sunny and warm, in sharp contrast to the cold, wintry view on the other side of the windows. Jemma fastened Melissa in her highchair and turned to retrieve a bottle from the refrigerator to place in the warmer. She smiled to discover that neighborly elves had left a pan of fresh cinnamon rolls on the stove top, and the coffee maker was in the process of brewing her morning energy drink. "Missy, your sweet Uncle Virgil and Aunt Cat have brought goodies. I'm sure they'll be coming back to see you after your morning nap. When you wake up, we'll get you bathed and dressed in your new red pants outfit … maybe a matching bow in your hair … if you won't pull it out."

It was approaching nine o'clock when Jemma returned Melissa to her crib and offered her a pacifier. "You rest while Mama takes a shower and gets dressed. Then, when you wake up, we'll get you ready and give Uncle Virgil and Aunt Cat a call and tell them you are ready to receive company." Jemma closed the door softly while adding, "Sweet dreams. I love you." She was pleased to see Missy yawn as her drowsy eyes blinked with sleepiness.

Without delay, Jemma gathered her clothes and prepared for a shower. She would clean Missy's tray and put the breakfast dishes away, then check to be sure the baby was asleep before she entered the bath herself. She never wanted to leave her child unattended for more than a few minutes, even though all safety precautions were in place.

Jemma dressed in a warm gray sweatsuit and rewrapped a towel around her damp hair. Melissa was still asleep, and Jemma covered her with the light blanket the baby had kicked off while stirring. As she lingered to absorb the beauty of innocent sleep, her cell phone began ringing, and she hurried to retrieve it from the desk in her bedroom. The caller I. D. indicated it was "Stella Abrams."

"Good morning, Stella. How are you? I hope you are calling with some good news," Jemma chirped.

"Jemma, I need to meet with you as soon as possible. When would be a convenient time?"

"Well, I'm off today. You can come anytime. Is everything okay?" Jemma could feel her chest tighten with anxiety.

"I'll explain when I get there. About thirty minutes?" she asked.

"Sure, that's fine." The connection ended.

Jemma robotically finished drying her hair, braided it loosely, and applied a bit of lipstick and mascara. She exchanged her house shoes for warm socks and running shoes, before making a quick survey of the house to ensure everything was in good order before the social worker arrived. It seemed Stella made quick time regardless of the weather—she was soon at the door ringing the bell.

"Come in, Stella." Gesturing toward a comfortable chair before the coffee table, Jemma said, "Please, have a seat." She noted only a brief, slight smile eased the serious composure of Mrs. Abram's face and demeanor.

"Thanks," Stella replied, then immediately continued: "Jemma, we have a problem with proceeding with the adoption. An attorney for the tribal council has appealed the termination of rights and your custody of Melissa, until DNA testing can prove her nationality. That means, of course, not only the adoption is in jeopardy, but your right as her legal guardian."

Choking on a sob, Jemma blurted, "But how can that be? What right … what has the tribe to do with anything?"

"Apparently someone has questioned Melissa's nationality—her genetics. I don't know who that might have been—a nurse, someone in the foster family— though highly unlikely. Perhaps, it was just someone who in the course of conversation questioned her being Hispanic. We don't know, but we are now required to have genetic testing. If Melissa proves to be Native American, even in part, she will be removed from your guardianship and placed with either a member of her biological family, if one can be located, or with an adoptive family in the Native American nation filing the appeal. It's the law, recently upheld by the Supreme Court."

"But what can we do?" Her voice struggled with anxiety. How could she, a single adoptive mother, defend her child—and herself, from an entire nation and the laws of her own country?

"As of now, we can only comply with the legal procedures outlined. We will provide the required DNA sample and wait for the result. I don't know how long that will take—days, weeks. Even if the test results are not in your favor, I will work to keep Melissa in your foster care until authorities find a willing biological relative or an approved adoptive Native American family.

Tears streamed down Jemma's face and left damp spots on the gray sweatshirt. "I can't believe this is happening. We never could have imagined ..."

Stella interrupted: "Jemma, you have provided a wonderful start for a precious little girl. If at some point she must leave, you have the blessed memory and experience of loving and nurturing her. And you and Seth will be getting married in a few months. Before long, you will bring another baby into that magical place you and Catherine have made. The pain you are feeling may intensify if all does not go as you pray it will. But your wedding, eventually another child ...  time, can ease the hurt of Melissa's loss."

"Perhaps. All I can do is pray. I know it's in God's hands. Excuse me, I must get a tissue." As Jemma moved toward her bedroom, she heard Melissa's babbling and went to scoop the child up in her arms. Holding her close, Jemma's tears washed the baby's cheek. Pulling away from Jemma, Melissa looked at her mother and patted her face. "Thank you, Missy. I love you, sweet baby."

Stella Abrams entered the nursery as Jemma was changing the baby's diaper. "I hope you don't mind my following you—I wanted to see this lovely nursery again."

Jemma held the wiggly child in place with one hand and took a tissue from the shelf and wiped her face and nose. "Not at all. You are always welcome in Melissa's world," Jemma replied with a sniff. "I must call Uncle Virgil and Aunt Catherine soon and tell them what's happening … not that there's anything they can do. But we can all pray for the best."

Stella came to Jemma's side and asked, "Do you mind if I hold Melissa?"

"No, not at all. She's nice and dry." Jemma lifted Melissa and transferred her to Stella's waiting arms.

"This is such a cuddly age. She's a beautiful child … and heavy. She must be a good eater," Stella observed.

"Yes, she's not picky at all and is right on schedule with her solid foods." Jemma chuckled: "Full disclosure—Uncle Virgil has been known to let her gum a pinch of cinnamon roll topping from time to time. They both enjoy that misbehavior." Jemma reached for another tissue, as she choked on her words: "He will be devastated if we lose her."

# Chapter 30

Catherine rested her hand on the rugged, heavy-knuckled hand of her husband, as he wiped tears pooling in his eyes. "I should have thought about that possibility," he grieved. "I know the tribe has rights over their children, but I was so enthralled with the notion of Melissa, I never once questioned her nationality. The woman said she was Hispanic—she was Hispanic."

"And, Virgil," Catherine consoled, "she may be. We won't know for sure until the testing is completed."

Melissa smacked her mouth with the sweetness of the cinnamon topping, as she sat on Jemma's lap and leaned against her chest. "I have had the deepest physical ache since Stella  told me. I just don't understand how justice is served to take a child away from the love and care of a good family—I mean, the child's own mother gave away her rights! What difference do genetics and skin color make?"

Catherine explained: "From what I've read, there is concern for the child's education in his native language and culture—an effort to maintain the tribal identity and heritage."

"Yes," added Virgil, "but I've heard there are family situations where a caring mother denies her nationality, simply wanting to get her child out of an abusive or dysfunctional environment that has nothing to do with culture and heritage. I'd get Missy the best Native American teacher I could find, to give her an appreciation of her heritage … to learn the language … if she could just stay in our care. Who knows what kind of family might end up taking her?"

"We just have to pray for whatever is best, whatever is God's will." Catherine's voice was soft, seeking to offer comfort and assurance.

Jemma appreciated her effort and knew Catherine was right, but she couldn't believe God's will included losing the heart that would be ripped from her with the loss of this child.

She sighed, "I've got to tell Seth. We'll go by the office and see if we can take him to lunch."

Virgil responded, "He's not in the office today. He woke up with a fierce headache this morning and said he'd rest and maybe go in this afternoon. He had a few pain pills left—he was taking one as we walked out the door. He said he had some paperwork he could work on at home when he got to feeling better."

Catherine added, "You might check on him while we're away from the house. We're going to be at Ethan's until later this evening. Cal's coming in from college, and we're celebrating his birthday."

"Sure," Jemma agreed. "I'll give him a call later ... see if he needs anything ... maybe take him some food."

"He'd like that for sure. You're always his best medicine." Catherine grasped Jemma's arm, adding, "And he, yours, I know."

Jemma smoothed strands of hair from her face and sighed: "Well, what is it you say ... 'Do what you can, pray, and stay busy'?"

"Maybe you two can start thinking about setting a date," Catherine suggested, "if he's feeling better and you are in a frame of mind to talk about wedding plans. The sooner you can look beyond today's clouds, the sooner you'll see tomorrow's rainbows."

Jemma smiled at another of Catherine's homespun sayings. "We'll see. But won't there be rain, if not storms, between the clouds and rainbows?" Wrapping her arms around Melissa to contain their bond, she added, "Right now, all I want is for both of us to be in one of Seth's big hugs."

Jemma and Melissa watched as Virgil and Catherine made their way cautiously across the snow-covered drive to the waiting truck. Jemma was amazed that inclement weather rarely deterred these Coyotes—back in Tennessee, the weatherman's prediction of "wintry precipitation" could clear store shelves and close schools.

"Well, sweet Missy, let's call Seth and see if he feels like a visit." Retrieving her phone from the kitchen table, Jemma called the number, anticipating the welcome sound of his voice. When there was no answer, she said, "Let's go do a diaper check. Then we'll try again. He may be sleeping."

Jemma was putting away the diapering supplies when the phone rang. "Ah, Missy, I bet that's Seth calling us back." Without noting the caller I. D., Jemma said, "Hello there, how are you feeling?"

"Well, really, rather well. I trust you and Melissa are warm this cold Wyoming day," the voice replied.

"Oh … Keeton?"

"The same."

"I was expecting a return call from Seth."

"I'm sorry to disappoint you. But, knowing today is your day off, I was wondering if I might drop by on my way to the gallery and see you and Melissa for a few minutes."

Jemma's thoughts whirled in the process of overcoming aversion to his visit and reasoning a potential benefit. Perhaps Keeton knew something about tribal affairs and customs—he obviously had a relationship with the people for some reason, if only for the proximity necessitated by his artwork. "Well, yes, that would be fine. I'm trying to arrange a time to take Seth some food. He's not feeling well and took a sick day, but I think he may be sleeping right now."

"Great. I'm not far from there, if soon is convenient?"

"Sure. Melissa's wide awake and in a good mood."

"Thanks so much. See you."

Jemma set Melissa before the nursery mirror, brushed her thick baby curls, and reclipped the red bow. *No wonder Keeton Fox is taken with her*, she thought. *He's an artist with a discerning eye for beauty.* Jemma restrained more tears, as she leaned to kiss the top of Missy's head and declared, "I'll do my best to go through the legal challenges of any nation that stands between you and me, sweet baby. Mama loves you."

Jemma and Melissa answered the ring of the doorbell. "Hello, Keeton, come in."

"Thank you," he replied, as he stomped snow on the thick entryway mat, then shed his boots and placed them in the boot tray inside the doorway. He stuffed his gloves in a pocket of the coat he removed and hung on the adjacent rack. He asked, "Are you getting used to the necessary inconveniences of wintry Wyoming?"

"I think so. I'm loving it—as long as I can stay inside by the fire and read an interesting book." She was surprised when Melissa leaned from her arms to reach out to Keeton.

"Hey, sweet girl, how lovely you look today in your pretty red bow—the perfect color for a special, excellent child." He took Melissa in his arms and gave her a kiss on the cheek. "I think she relates to me as the only other dark-haired, brown-eyed creature in her world—besides her Teddy bear, of course."

"I hadn't thought of that," Jemma responded. "I was a bit sensitive to the fact she was so willing to leave my arms. Have a seat and warm yourself by the fire."

"Thanks, Jemma." Settling himself in the armchair, with Melissa on his lap, Keeton declared: "How comfortable and pleasant this is!"

"Would you like to give Melissa her bottle? She had a late breakfast and snacked on cinnamon roll topping earlier. She won't be ready for lunch for a while, but I'm sure she would enjoy some milk … well, formula, actually."

"I'd like that, if you don't mind," he answered.

Jemma returned from the kitchen and gave him the bottle, which Melissa immediately seized with both hands.

When all three were settled for conversation, Jemma questioned: "Keeton, how much knowledge do you have of the Native American tribes in the area? I know you have some insight—your paintings reflect your love and understanding of the people."

Hesitating for a few seconds, he answered: "My father is Crow—Joseph Whitefox. My mother was never able to settle into my father's world and divorced him when I was seven. I remained with him on the reservation until I left to pursue art study. My father was not happy about that, to say the least, but he felt the only way to keep me was to set me free … a wise man. He has been pleased with my representation of our people through my painting. But," he smiled, "you understand that." He looked at Melissa and adjusted the bottle before continuing: "I lived with my mother in Billings during college. I have continued to live in her house since her death. So, I am well acquainted with all things Crow—or rather, the

Apsáalooke. They are in my genes and in my heart, though I have been in the outside world for years. To be an artist was my passion, but the heart of that passion was my people, my heritage."

For some moments, Jemma digested the information Keeton had just revealed. "Thanks, Keeton, I find your words comforting. This has been a difficult, disruptive morning." Jemma related to him the news of Stella Abram's visit, the required genetic testing, and the possible subsequent removal of Melissa from her home. Tears welled in her eyes again as she declared, "Her loss would be the hardest thing I have ever experienced. All I can do is pray for what is best for her … and trust that, somehow, it's best for me too."

"Man's law changes with his understanding of man. Only the laws of the spirit remain always the same," he quoted. "I'm not sure who said that or even what "the understanding of man" means. Do the emotional and physical interests of the child trump preservation of culture and heritage, or vice-versa? As a *'half-breed'* myself," he smirked, "I see validity in both sides of the issue. … But I do know, if testing confirms her Native American ancestry, the tribal council will be successful in its appeal and attaining custody—due not only to the law, but to the current societal and political pressures. "

"Well … thank you for your honesty. I know I must try to prepare for the worst … but I can't prepare for not knowing where she is, how she is …"

He interrupted: "Jemma, if you should lose on the appeal, if possible, I'll try to learn of her placement and seek to be some connection between you and the child. If it is in my power, she always will know of your love for her and your concern for her well-being and happiness."

"Thank you, Keeton. That is so much appreciated."

Surprising herself, she smiled and declared: "I think you may become a true friend—not just a professional friend."

"Well, that's good to hear. I hope so. Jemma, let me assure you, that's all I've ever wanted—a friend who appreciates and understands my work, who connects with the soul that communicates through it.  For whatever reason, I've felt some strange tension of dislike or distrust between us since our first encounter at the gallery. I have wondered what I might have said or done to get off on the wrong footing with you."

"Honestly," Jemma admitted, "that was a stressful time for me—a time of recovering from an unhealthy relationship. Every man was red-flagged. No offense, but you reminded me of the cad I left behind in Tennessee— charming, smooth …"

"Well, I like the sound of 'charming," but 'smooth" sounds manipulative …"

"Exactly—so I was immediately defensive. Perhaps, an apology is in order. You've always been courteous and more than gracious, and at times I may have been rude."

"Oh, no, I wouldn't say that—just … more guarded." With a sly smile, he confessed, "I know I have a reputation as the dark, inscrutable artist—likely, a womanizer." He shrugged. "I let it be—seems to help sales."

Jemma laughed for the first time in the difficult day: "I would say 'materialistic' is a fitting descriptive."

"Oh, yes, definitely," he agreed. "Dark? Obviously. Inscrutable? More just personally reserved, engaged in the artist's world of solitary pursuits. Womanizer? Well, I appreciate beauty and intelligence in any woman, but I gave my heart and allegiance to my wife, and I've never reneged."

Jemma was shocked. "Your wife? I've never heard you have a wife."

"Only a few people know. She's young. She comes and goes as she pleases. Her father was abusive … I think she has PTSD. She has a bad taste for my life here and my work—she stays away much of the time. Like my father let me go, I let her go. I make sure she has what she needs … she knows her home is with me when she wants it." He lowered his gaze to Melissa.

For the first time, Jemma saw Keeton as an honest man—a man in pain. *Perhaps*, she thought, *that's the emotional overtone of his work.* "Two Worlds," she blurted. "That's your wife."

"Yes," he replied softly. "That was the last time she told me she had to get away. I didn't understand how our love could not heal her pain, make everything all right. But I knew I had to trust that love to hold us together, even when we were apart. So …" He shook his head as if flicking away a pesty thought. "It's satisfying to know the painting is here, with you, in a safe and love-filled place, just as I hope, wherever Kalie is, she feels secure and knows she is loved." After a few seconds of silence, Keeton added: "Well, this certainly has been a morning of revelation—'spilling one's guts,' to use that rather coarse definition."

Dabbing an eye, Jemma noted, "She's fallen sound asleep. I'll take her and put her in bed."

"Do you mind if I just sit here and hold her? She seems comfortable enough."

"She surely does. No, I don't mind. I'll check on Seth. Would you like anything—coffee, water, a sandwich, a cinnamon roll?" Jemma asked.

"No, thanks, I'm fine."

"Okay, I'll be right back." Jemma went to the

kitchen to call. She frowned when there was no answer. Returning to the living room, she stated: "Keeton, if you can stay with Melissa for just a bit, I'm going to over to Virgil and Catherine's. Seth is not answering, and I'm a bit concerned. They said he had a fierce headache this morning, and he may not be completely out of the woods after his brain injury."

"No problem. We'll be right here when you get back." He raised a two-fingered sign and said, "Friend."

Jemma smiled, made the sign in response, and said, "Yes."

Jemma donned her boots and winter gear and hurried across the street. When the doorbell and knocking failed to get a response, she took the emergency key from the faux rock container near the walkway and entered the house. "Seth?" she called, but there was no answer. The door to his bedroom was open. "Seth?" She entered to find Seth lying on the floor next to the bed—he was barely conscious and unresponsive.

## Chapter 31

The ambulance siren was fading in the distance when Catherine and Virgil pulled into the driveway of their home. Jemma, waiting on the porch, rushed to them and leaned into their embrace. "It's not good," she sobbed. "It's not good." Pulling away, she cried, "Melissa … I've got to get back to Melissa."

"Where is she?" Catherine's question was stressed, urgent.

"Keeton is watching her, but I have to get back."

"Keeton?" Virgil queried. Then he directed, "Come, dear. We'll go home with you." Virgil put his arm around Jemma and guided her back across the street.

Meeting them at the door with Melissa, awake and still in his arms, Keeton implored: "I've been nearly frantic. What's happened?"

Taking Melissa from him, Jemma hugged the child tightly against her and answered: "I'm guessing Seth has had a brain bleed from his old injury—or, possibly, a stroke. He's unconscious." Jemma's face felt swollen, tight—cold with frosted tears. "He was alive but unresponsive when they loaded him in the ambulance."

Virgil stated, "Catherine, stay here with Melissa, and Jemma and I will go to the hospital."

"Surely," she responded, taking the child from Jemma. "She's likely ready for her lunch."

Jemma extended her hand to Keeton. "Thank you for your help."

Placing his hand over hers, he said, smiling, "That's what friends are for."

"Yes. Friends are important." Her response was

flat, with emotions overwhelmed and stymied by the challenges of the day.

Keeton donned his boots and outerwear, while directing his words to Virgil: "I'll call this evening to check on Seth's status. If you need anything, anything at all, please don't hesitate to ask. I'll be in town a couple of days."

"Thanks, Keeton. We'll stay in touch." Virgil kissed Catherine, bussed Missy's cheek, and asked, "Jemma, you ready?" He waited for her to cup Missy's face in her hands and declare, "Mama loves you, sweet girl."

The ICU floor was quiet except for the rhythmic percussion of machines, monitoring life functions and pumping meds and oxygen to patients in the neurocritical unit. Virgil stayed in the family waiting room while Jemma registered at the nurses' station, then took her place behind the glass wall of Seth's private room. She observed as one of her colleagues adjusted tubing, took Seth's vitals, and recorded her measurements and stats from machines that had more apparent life than Seth's now comatose being. She noted, as she had expected, he was ventilated.

"Miss Garrison—or should I say, 'Nurse Garrison'?" came the familiar voice of Dr. Hassam. "I understand you are Mr. Clay's fiancée."

"Yes. I found him unconscious in his apartment when I couldn't reach him by phone, and he didn't answer the door."

"Do you have any idea how long he was unconscious?" he asked.

"No, it could have been a few minutes, or it could have been over two hours. He lives in an apartment in my aunt and uncle's house. They saw him in the kitchen taking pain medication when they left. He told them he had a fierce headache and was going to stay home from work. That was … maybe … around 8:30 or 9:00, and I found him about 11:00 … I really don't know for sure. I wasn't noticing the time."

"I see." He made some notes on the chart in his hand, pushed his glasses up his nose, and continued: "I don't have to tell you his condition is critical. I venture to say he was unconscious not long after your aunt and uncle saw him, when he had what we sometimes call a 'thunderclap' headache. I have ordered an EEG. Honestly, I am not expecting the results to be encouraging. I'm sorry."

Jemma wiped the continuous flow of tears from her face. "I understand. Thank you. May I go in briefly?"

"Yes, for a moment."

"My uncle—he's been a father to Seth—may he see him also?"

"Yes, but only for a moment."

"Thank you."

Jemma entered the sterile glass package containing monitors and Seth's long still form. Ventilator tubing was taped to his mouth, and the recurring *whoosh-thump-thump* sound, though familiar, had never seemed so foreboding. She held his hand in hers and pressed it to her lips. "I love you, Seth. I'm going to get Virgil so he can see you. We'll be right back."

Scurrying to the waiting room, she drew Virgil's attention, as he watched the door in anticipation of news. "Come," she mouthed and motioned. As they moved down the hall, she said, "The doctor said we can have a few moments with him. They are going to do an EEG to check his brain activity. Dr. Hassam thinks he may have been unconscious a significant amount of time." Reaching to hold Virgil's hand, she continued, "The doctor is not optimistic."

Virgil choked on a sob as he entered Seth's room and saw him, motionless, his very existence dependent on the machines surrounding him. Together they walked to the bedside. Virgil's massive hand grasped Seth's. Tears coursed over his lips as he spoke: "Seth, Seth, I love you. Don't leave us, son."

The nurse reentered the room. "I'm sorry. I must ask you to leave. We are going to run some tests. If you'd like to return to the waiting room, Dr. Hassam will report to you if and when he has any information."

Virgil gripped Seth's hand as Jemma leaned over to give Seth a kiss. She wondered if it would be the last.

Styrofoam coffee cup in hand, Jemma stood at the window of the waiting room and watched the snow falling around the lampposts, glowing in the darkness of the early evening sky. She turned to see her uncle had dozed off in a recliner provided for heart and body-weary family members like them. *How fast a day can change!* she thought. She had awakened with joy and thankfulness for a day of cozy warmth with her daughter; now, she was trying to survive the remaining hours with strength of faith and prayer—and lots of dark, strong coffee. She knew the caffeine was increasing her nervous restlessness, but it also kept her awake, alert, and focused on … what? Waiting … wondering?

"Garrison family?" the nurse called, and Jemma rushed to the sound of her voice, responding, "Here!" Uncle Virgil roused from his sleep and pushed down the foot of the recliner to stand and join Jemma as she passed.

They met the nurse at the door. She directed: "If

you will follow me, please, back to Mr. Clay's room, Dr. Hassam has some information for you."

Hassam was flipping through the pages of Seth's chart, making notes as he did. After years of nursing, she knew doctors' faces were usually hard to read, but there was something about body language and the apparent absorption with charting that seemed to indicate whether they expected their interaction with relatives would be well-received or uncomfortably emotional. She didn't like what was registering in her medical mind.

"Miss Garrison, Mr. Garrison," he nodded as they approached. After one last note, he closed the chart cover and stated: "I'm sorry I must inform you that Mr. Clay's test results were not good. He apparently developed a brain bleed, likely as a result of the TBI several weeks ago. After he reported the terrible headache this morning, he likely lost consciousness and fell within a few minutes. He apparently had intracranial bleeding for quite some time. His EEG showed significant brain damage … minimal activity. We will keep him on life support for 48 hours. If there is no improvement in that time, you will need to make the decision to remove support or to arrange to move him to life care nursing. I am really deeply sorry."

Jemma melted into Virgil's arms, and he rested his chin on her head, his tears dampening her hair.

"Nurse," the doctor called. "See to helping them. They may need to contact family or friends … get transportation … whatever." He took a prescription pad from his shirt, scratched a note with his signature, and handed it to her: "See they have some Ativan on hand if needed."

"Yes, doctor."

He turned back as he left. "Let them have as much time with him as they want the next couple of days—

within those stretchable hospital regulations, of course," he added.

In the waiting room, hand in hand, the two people in the world nearest in heart to Seth Clay sat silently, allowing the full import of Hassam's words to penetrate their clouded minds. Jemma could see the weariness in Virgil's face and body, and she knew he needed rest and the comfort of his bed and Catherine's care. Jemma's call to her had been brief and to the point, leaving Catherine sobbing. She was glad her aunt was occupied with Melissa, though now it was well past time for the baby to be settled in her bed and asleep.

She strained to force her intellect and nursing expertise to overcome her own ravaged emotions. She knew they both required food and recharging if they were to be by Seth's side as they desired the next couple of days. "Uncle Virgil, let's go home for a while. There's nothing we can do here, and we'll want to come back early in the morning. Let me have the truck keys, and I'll drive us home."

"Virgil? Jemma?" The figure of Keeton Fox shadowed the soft light from the overhead fixture.

"Keeton?" Jemma questioned.

He continued: "I hope you don't mind my intrusion. I'm staying at the inn only a couple of blocks from here. I wanted to see if I can be of help. I called Catherine who told me the prognosis, and I can't tell you how I grieve for you both."

"Thank you, Keeton," Jemma replied.

"Yes, thanks. Kind of you," Virgil added, not raising his head.

"I was just telling Uncle Virgil we need to go home and get some rest before coming back in the morning.

We'll be leaving soon."

"Let me drive you," their friend offered.

"We have Uncle Virgil's truck. I can drive," she stated.

"Jemma, neither one of you is in any condition to drive, especially in this weather. Let me take you home. If you feel up to it in the morning, you can come back in your car, and Virgil can pick up his truck tomorrow."

Jemma stared at Keeton, trying to focus and assess the circumstances, then lowered her head and answered, "You're right. Thanks for the offer." She helped Virgil into his coat, donned her own gear, and took her bag from the floor under her seat. *A man who has friends must himself be friendly*. How strange that familiar scriptures popped into her head: *Yet who knows whether you have come into our lives for such a time as this?*"

# Chapter 32

"Jemma, please eat something. I'm sure you haven't had a bite of food since yesterday morning." Catherine's persuasion caused her to take a biscuit and spoon some scrambled egg from the pan on the stove.

Sitting at the kitchen table with her plate and coffee cup, she reported: "I'm taking a few days' leave. I thought I'd drop Melissa off at the nursery, so you can go with us to the to the hospital. If you like, when you're ready to leave, you can take my car with the baby seat and pick up Missy on the way home."

"That's a good plan. I want to see Seth, but I don't want to leave Melissa in day care more than necessary." As she covered a plate of food, she continued: "I left Virgil asleep, so I'll take him some food. It was early this morning before he finally crashed in his lounger."

After a bite of food, Jemma pushed her plate away and declared: "I must be living on auto-pilot. I can't think. I can't feel. Even your food has no taste—it's just something in my mouth that threatens to choke me."

Catherine moved to hug Jemma toward her aproned body and kissed the top of her head. "My poor Jemma. You can do this—you will survive. God will not put on us more than we're able to bear ... though you may doubt that until you come out alive on the other side of this seemingly endless dark day."

"It seems I can't hold onto any happiness in my life. First, Cory—though that was just an illusion. Now, Seth ... and, if I lose Melissa ..." Jemma wiped her nose with the napkin near her plate. "And I am being pitifully self-centered—I don't even like myself."

"Jemma, it's okay to feel like this—for a time anyway. But you must think of others—the blessings they have brought … and the blessings you have been and can be to them. You have given your uncle and me so much joy. You have given Melissa a wonderful start in a home full of love and comfort. And, as for Seth, he thought he would never again know peace and contentment after his loss of Rachel and the baby. He has been happy and hopeful these last several months—because of you."

Jemma wrapped her arms around Catherine and pressed her head against apron pockets collecting her tears. "Thank you. I love you."

"I love you too, dear." Catherine smoothed Jemma's hair and added, "Jemma, now is the time to put your faith to work. If and when the time comes for Seth to leave this world, you can know he is with Rachel and his son. He will have joy beyond measure. You must have faith that, with hope and patience, you will find joy and contentment yourself."

Jemma sat erect at the sound of Melissa's cry. "There's a joyful sound. I'll change her diaper and feed her some breakfast—make that, have her join me for breakfast. One foot in front of the other, I can do this," she smiled weakly.

"I know you can, Jemma," Catherine reassured her.


Thankfully, the sun gave a sense of warmth on the frigid day of burial. Melissa's head rested quietly on Jemma's shoulder. The child was tired after the commotion of the previous evening when the family arrived—Jemma's parents and Laurie with Stan, now her fiancé. Seth had not survived the 48-hour period the doctor had indicated, and in the family's immediate prayer upon receiving news of his passing, Virgil had given thanks that Seth had not lingered in the comatose state—that the family would not field any request or feel pressured to "pull the plug."

Jemma heard the preacher's words of tribute to Seth and his expressions of consolation to friends and family, but her mind and focus wandered—to the Bighorns, strung in regal procession beyond the graveyard, to the markers that declared the nearby interments of "Rachel Bloodman Clay" and "Infant Son, Virgil"—to the faces and reactions of friends and family encircling the casket, many of whom were watching her and analyzing her reactions. She nodded with appreciation to the covey of nurses who had come to support her. Near them was Stella Abrams and, she assumed, Stella's husband, Richard—and Virgil's floor manager, Connie White. To her surprise, she recognized Tess, the young girl from the trading post. Considering the attendance at the funeral and now the throng who followed Seth's body to its grave, he had left behind positive, even sweet memories of his kind and generous heart. Of course, many were there out of respect for Virgil Garrison and awareness that Seth was the "son" he had groomed to be heir of Garrison Emporium. Jemma was confident they, like she, wondered what Virgil would do now without Seth.

Jemma's gaze was drawn to the person standing a few feet behind the immediate circle. Keeton Fox caught her attention and raised the familiar two-fingered sign, to which Jemma mouthed, "Thank you."

The knock on the nursery door was soft, obviously careful not to disturb a sleeping child. "Come in," Jemma responded. "She's totally out—worn to a frazzle by family and friends bringing food."

Virgil entered hesitantly and, pointing to the footstool, asked, "Mind if I sit?"

"No, not at all." Wistfully, Jemma added, "That was Seth's spot when he'd come to visit. That's where he proposed to me."

"Ah, Jemma, there is a huge hole in my heart," he sighed.

"I know. My entire future is now one big hole I'm not sure how to fill."

"Jemma, it's early to be thinking about that future, but these have been thoughts in the quiet times today. I just want to tell you what I've wondered, questioned, considered—whatever you want to call it. And I don't want you to think me heartless for even thinking about such things. But Seth was my son in every way that counts—my heir, my business partner, my friend … my future nephew," he smiled poignantly.

Jemma said, "Uncle Virgil, I could never ever think you heartless. You know you can be open with me."

"Well …" He sought the right words. "I was thinking, if I were you, there would be a ton of painful memories attached to that hospital. I don't know how much nursing is a *love* or a *calling* to you, or if it is simply a good way to make a living at something you find rewarding. But, if you had any interest at all, I believe you would have a mind and aptitude for running Garrison Emporium. I would love to see you sitting at that same desk Seth was occupying—I would have every confidence in you to care for the business—to learn it and run it just as adeptly as he was."

"Oh, Uncle Virgil, I don't know," she protested. "I've never had any experience running a business, except for being a cashier for Dad during summer breaks."

"Well, like I said, I probably shouldn't even think

about business right now, but it's been weighing on my mind." He reached out and patted her hand. "Now, I'll let it weigh on yours a bit."

## Chapter 33

"I'm sorry, Jemma." A stack of files stood apparently untouched on the corner of Stella Abram's desk, while the documents from the "Garrison Baby" folder were fanned across the desk calendar in front of her. "The DNA test indicates Melissa is fifty percent Native American. She is not eligible for legal custody or adoption outside the Crow Nation, the ones making the appeal."

Jemma took some deep breaths before speaking: "I've tried to prepare myself for those words." Her well of tears had run dry days ago. She rubbed her forehead and sighed, "What now?"

"Well, I'm still working with Roger Burnham to see if we can keep Melissa in your temporary care until placement is found. I see no reasonable need to move her to another, interim foster home before the search is complete."

"Do you have any idea how long placement will take?" she asked.

"No, it depends on how quickly the biological family can be located, if it can be. If a willing relative is found, she will be moved as soon as the receiving home can provide accommodation; if not, she will be placed with an approved adoptive family or in foster care according to the ICWA regulations. As I said, I am hoping to maintain temporary care with you."

"Will there be any trials or court proceedings in which we'll be involved?" Jemma asked.

"No, I don't believe so. As a foster care provider, you really have no legal grounds on which to contest the appeal—none that would have any chance of surviving.

I'm guessing a judge will sign off on the petition, and you will receive a notice or call with a date on which to have Melissa ready for pick up, along with any belongings and supplies you want to relinquish. That day the attending officers will provide you with a warrant for her surrender."

Jemma scrutinized the folded hands lying in her lap and processed the information for some seconds. Then, she observed: "Love for the child seems to get lost all in the legalities." Raising her head and steeling her resolve, she continued: "Stella, I appreciate so much all the effort you have made on our behalf. You are a capable and caring worker. I know you truly are concerned about those you represent."

"Well, thank you for those words. I find my work rewarding when outcomes are what we want. But I am bound by the constraints of the law, which sometimes seems to have lost its heart in the quest for justice." Stella brushed the papers back into their folder. "There is this, Jemma: Melissa … or whatever her legal name may be … she is very young. Her memory of the transition … the emotional toll on her …that should be minimal and short-lived. Very young children, thankfully, are good forgetters. But you, friend, are going to have some difficult days ahead. I hope your hurt can be eased by many future good things that come to you."

"Thanks, Stella," Jemma responded, as she picked up her bag and stood to leave.

"I'll keep you informed as soon as I know of any movement in the process," Stella stated. Then she asked, "Do you have any immediate plans? You're not thinking about going back to Tennessee, are you?"

"Oh, no," Jemma answered, "not for more than just a visit. For better or worse, I'm settled here. I have the house … much more than enough house … and Uncle

Virgil and Aunt Catherine nearby. I've decided not to return to the hospital, to nursing, but to try my hand at managing the Emporium. Uncle Virgil assures me I can learn the ropes—and that I mean literally," she said with a brief smile. "I'm praying that will keep my mind occupied … distracted … when Melissa's gone."

"I think that's a great idea." Stella stood as she said, "Even when there are no sad personal circumstances associated with it, the hospital is not a place to promote happy thoughts and sweet dreams." She reached to take Jemma's hand and sandwiched it between her own. "You will be in my thoughts."

"Thank you," Jemma concluded. She stood to make her way out of the office toward the entrance of the building. She remembered the hope and excitement she had felt the first time she had walked these halls and wondered if there was anything that might return to her the optimism of that day.

Passing the nursery center on the way to the Emporium, she thought, *Melissa would have enjoyed 'school' there two or three days a week—the friends, the educationally-enriched environment.* But no 'keeper' could surpass Catherine in love and attention. Her aunt would grieve to learn Missy's loss was imminent. … and Uncle Virgil … well, remembering her conversation with Seth about broken heart syndrome, she didn't want to think about the effect Stella's news might have on him at his age and stage of health. Jemma determined, if he was in the office as she expected, she would ask him out to lunch—a bison burger, of course—and pass the information to him as tactfully and gently as possible.

Jemma took pleasure in the office she had cleaned

and organized to her satisfaction—not that her uncle and Seth had been inordinately messy, but she brought "a woman's touch." And still a nurse with a perfectionist's mindset, she knew she could think and learn better in an uncluttered environment where everything had "its place."

Uncle Virgil had left evidence that he was present somewhere in the building: lying on the desk was one of Seth's books about Wyoming wildlife, opened to the chapter, "Coyotes—Behaviors and Native Legends." She swept her hands over the cool, smooth pages, knowing Seth had touched and turned them. Taking the volume and deciding to occupy herself while waiting for Virgil, she nestled in the brown leather executive's chair and read: "Coyotes are social animals, living in stable packs with a definite hierarchical system of organization. Alpha males and females, usually the oldest and strongest, are solely responsible for reproduction. Beta males and females have supporting roles, beta males acting as 'sidekicks' in the Alpha male's quest for food, and Beta females, as secondary mothers to the Alpha female's pups." Jemma slammed the book, shutting out the offensive words, and returned it to the nearby bookcase. Her hope—her desire and expectation, to be a wife and mother, an "Alpha female," had vanished with the loss of Seth. Now, even her longing and plan to be a nurturing, supportive "Beta female" were in jeopardy.

"Whoa, did you drop something?" Virgil asked as he appeared at the doorway with a newspaper under his arm.

"No, just closing the book you left on the desk—a little too forcefully, I guess."

"What did that poor book do to you?" he teased, taking a seat in one of the armchairs. Assessing Jemma's moment of silent expression, he continued, "Jemma, what's wrong? Did the meeting with Stella go badly?"

Jemma stationed her elbows on the table and rested her chin on her clenched hands. "Yes, Uncle Virgil, just as we feared. I wanted to find a gentle way of telling you—not by slamming a book. But it simply 'is what it is.' Melissa's fifty percent Native American. Stella and the attorney are going to see if we may be allowed to keep her in foster care until the authorities can place her with a biological relative or adoptive family in the tribe."

"Oh, Jemma, this does hurt." He laid the Free Beacon on the desk, took a handkerchief from his jacket pocket, and wiped his eyes. "I can't say I expected anything else … but this confirmation makes it final—it's really going to happen."

"I have no idea how much time we'll have with her, but I want us to enjoy every moment," she declared.

"Yes, we will." Taking a deep breath, he exhaled and said, "I need to let Catherine know. Let's hold off on office duties and go home to her and the baby. I'll tell Connie she's in charge today. We'll go out to lunch, show off the baby, and find something fun to entertain her … maybe, the toy store over on Brundage. I think they've got their Christmas lights and decorations up already."

"That sounds good," Jemma responded, reaching for her coat and bag.

Virgil stood to leave, then turned back toward the desk. "I almost forgot. I don't want to be the bearer of more bad news but take a look at this." He opened the newspaper and pointed to the article in the lower right-hand corner. "Prominent local artist arrested for domestic disorderly conduct." Jemma was stunned by the appearance of Keeton Fox's picture below the disturbing headline.

# Chapter 34

Jemma had just pulled the new laptop from its box and had begun the process of setup when her cell phone began ringing impatiently. "Jemma, this is Keeton. I hope I haven't caught you at an inconvenient moment."

"Uh … hello, Keeton. No, I'm at the Emporium office, just getting ready to set up a new laptop, so I can access files on-the-go."

Fox's voice was raspy as he continued: "I suppose you are aware of the incident in Billings?"

"I did see the story in the Beacon. I must say I was shocked. The person in the report did not sound like the Keeton I thought I knew," she answered honestly.

"I'd like to explain what happened." She could sense hurt and pleading in his voice. "The newspaper report made the whole thing sound terrible, and I am embarrassed and humiliated. You must think me horrible."

"I won't know what to think until I hear your explanation," she replied. "Screaming at your wife and throwing her from the front porch … the neighbors calling the police … it doesn't sound good."

"The situation was considered a first offense misdemeanor, and the judge released me on my own recognizance. If Kalie doesn't have the charges dismissed, I will have to appear in court. But my concern is that you understand what happened. I'm coming into Sheridan to bring a piece to the gallery—and I have something for you. Would you be free and willing to meet me for coffee about ten this morning? If you think it might tarnish your reputation to be seen with a criminal, I understand completely."

"Oh, Keeton, not at all. Sure, I'll meet you. At the coffee shop near the gallery?"

"Yes, that will be fine … and … thank you, Jemma. See you there." He cut the connection.

Jemma checked her watch to see she had more than an hour until her meeting. She wondered how there could be any explanation for the behavior reported by the Billings news. It seemed totally out of character for Keeton, but she knew little about the strange off-and-on again relationship he had with his young wife, Kalie. Jemma did know he had been a friend to her at a difficult time, and surely, he needed the listening ear of a friend now.

Jemma entered the coffee shop to find Keeton sitting in a remote corner, away from curious eyes and ears. He looked exhausted and gaunt. His was not the usual persona of dapper artist, but that of haggard wretch, suffering the effects of hunger, sleeplessness, and anxiety. When he saw her, he stood to take her hand: "Jemma, thank you for coming."

Jemma could not restrain the response: "Keeton, you don't look well. Are you taking care of yourself?"

"That's typically considerate of you to ask. It seems I have little appetite, and my sleep is disturbed by one nightmare after another. … Anxiety? Not so much worry as regret and wishing I could erase the terrible decisions I've made."

"We all make unwise choices in our lives," she stated.

"Yes, but it seems the reality of mine and their consequences have all poured down on me at once."

"I'm here, Keeton, to listen and to help if I can." Jemma touched his arm, and he laid his hand on hers.

"Thanks. You are the only friend I know who seems to have the answers and direction I need right now." Keeton retrieved a sketch pad and pen from his jacket pocket, laid the tablet on the table, and began doodling. "You may think I've lost my mind, but sketching will help me to focus on my words."

Jemma waited in silence for Keeton to continue: "That evening, Kalie showed up at mother's house—our house. At previous times when she'd return, she'd be sweet … apologetic for staying away so long. She'd say she had missed me and wanted things to be good between us again. And, for a few days, they would be … then, she'd be gone … with enough funds to take up the slack in what she was able to make as a waitress. Sometimes she'd stay somewhere in Billings; at other times, she'd come down here to Sheridan and work. I thought about hiring a detective to follow her moves, but that seemed so sleazy … and I wanted to trust her. I loved her … I had helped her escape from her abusive father …  I knew … or thought I knew, our relationship, though unusual, was permanent and workable."

Jemma thought about the relationship she had escaped—it seemed providence was working on her behalf to help her see Cory's true character before she committed herself to him. That was a stressful time emotionally, but she might be suffering the same anxiety and sleepless nights as Keeton had the relationship survived. Yes, losing Seth was heartbreaking, and there was concern over Melissa's welfare, but she had a faith to guide her and a family to share her blessings and strengthen her in times of challenge and disappointment. Keeton needed not only her friendship, but her family and her faith.

"That night … the night of the argument, Kalie told me she was leaving and not coming back—that she had found 'the love of her life.' It was painful … but I must admit, there was little surprise—that was a scenario I had imagined. She never even sat down in the living room. She simply laid papers on the coffee table, saying, 'I got a divorce in Sheridan—it's quick and easy there.'"

Jemma noticed Keeton had sketched a picture of the Garrison house and grounds, much like that on the cake he had decorated all those months ago.

"All I could say was, 'Okay.' Can you believe that?" He raised tearful eyes to look at Jemma with a wry smile and continued: "Your wife tells you she is no longer your wife, and you say 'Okay'?" Keeton tore the sheet from the pad and began drawing again. "I did say, 'I'm thankful we have no children to suffer your abandonment.'" His drawing became faster, almost frantic.

"Keeton?" A tinge of fear was rising within her.

"Do you know what she said? Do you *know* what she told me?" Moisture glistened on his face, and he wiped his eyes with his shirt sleeve. "She said, 'No, I took care of that. I got rid of the baby.'" Keeton stabbed the tablet with his pen and dropped onto the table, his head on his folded arms.

"Oh, Keeton, no." Jemma put her arm around his shoulders and waited for him to compose himself.

After several moments, he concluded: "That's when I lost it. I screamed for her to get out. I grabbed her arm and flung her out the door. She stumbled and lost her footing and fell off the porch. She wasn't injured seriously—just a sprained ankle, I think. The next-door neighbor came out on his porch when he heard the commotion. The man that brought Kalie jumped out of his car and yelled at the neighbor to call the police. The rest is history, as they say—a police report and newspaper article.

But you … you have the context. I'm not excusing what I did, but I am explaining it."

Jemma struggled to find a response and words of consolation. She wondered how any reasonable woman could abort the human being developing within her: *Selfishness must far outweigh any connection to the child, to his father, or to the God of life.* She waited some time before speaking: "Keeton, you can survive this. You have your friends to help … my family … and your work." She picked up the sketch. "Just as you have poured your hurt and anger into this, throw all your pain and confusion into your art. Let it be a distraction, a release—a catharsis. Trust there will be better days ahead. You can choose to grovel in the destruction and misery of what is now 'history'—or you can try to clean up whatever mess and broken pieces are left behind and determine to make a new future for yourself."

Keeton picked up the pen and studied it before responding. "You are right. It's hard … but you are right." He chuckled: "You love the 'muted tones' of my watercolor work … but I may get the oils out again … with all the intense, fiery colors of anger and the ivory black of despondency. I can empty my heart and slather it thick and deep on the canvas. It can be Fox's 'Rage Phase.'"

Recognizing some humor in his sarcasm, she smirked, "Whatever works for you."

"I already have a record—a rap sheet. Maybe I can move on to felonies … if they're more profitable."

She prayed this attempt at levity was a first step on the other side of misery. "Always the shameless materialist," she teased. "You may find the newspaper article alone has increased interest in your work—maybe even its value. It seems every great artist has a colorful background—no pun intended."

"Clever," he remarked. I'll be using that one myself." Swiping his sleeve across his face and combing his hair out of his eyes with his fingers, he asked, "Do you mind if we go back to your office? I've got something I want to give you. I've made enough of a spectacle of myself here."

"Sure. I walked. I'll meet you down there."

"Do you mind if I walk with you?" he asked, as he wrapped a woolen scarf around his neck.

"Not at all. The cold air will do us both good," she declared, zipping her jacket and donning fleece-lined gloves.

"Did you make your delivery at the gallery?"

"Yes. I could have taken it to the gallery in Billings, but I've had a couple of early Christmas sales here, so I thought I'd restock. Besides, I'm considering selling the house and moving to Sheridan. I think the memories there will stifle my creativity. The Billings gallery exhibits and sells online. I'll just deliver to them occasionally as I've been doing with the gallery here."

"Well, give yourself time to think things through. That's your mother's house—your inheritance, I assume."

"Yes … and she was a loving person … perhaps a bit eccentric, but kind and generous. She encouraged me to paint—to find the passion that could motivate me to make it my life's occupation. Her recurring advice was, "If your passion is in your work, you'll never grow weary."

"A wise woman," Jemma stated, as they drew near the Emporium.

"I'm parked in the lot next door. I'll meet you at the office," he said.

"Straight through the first floor to the rear hallway. You'll see the sign."

Jemma removed her gloves and stuffed them into the pocket of her jacket, which she hung on the office hall tree. She put the computer box and accessories aside and had not yet taken a seat when Keeton knocked on the doorframe.

"Hey, come in," she greeted.

From behind him he pulled what she recognized as a wrapped canvas. "This is just a little something for my girl—the baby one," he added with a laugh.

"Keeton, what have you done? You are too generous." She took the package, unwrapped it, and sat down in the office chair. Her hand could not catch the simultaneous tears and sobs that escaped from her at the sight of the painting—the beauty and innocence of Melissa Jane, red bow in her brunette hair, brown eyes glinting with light, hands clasped with joy, and a precious baby smile, so hard to capture but worth the wait … for perfection. "It's wonderful" she whispered. "But how did you manage …"

"I trust this was something good—a 'blessing,' as you say—that came out of the morning of Seth's fatal fall. I made sketches of Melissa while I was with her at your house. She was happy and full of baby giggles—so beautiful … so totally untouched by anything but love and comfort. I hope I captured some of that in the painting."

"Oh, Keeton, yes … yes, you did. Thank you. It will be a precious treasure in my home."

"Well," he stammered, "I'm so pleased—and you are welcome. It was a work of joy."

As he turned to leave, Jemma added, "Keeton, thank you for loving Melissa." She teased, "You're so much better than a brown eyed Teddy bear."

He smiled before turning to leave, then, looking back, added, "Thank you, Jemma, for being my friend.

You may have even saved a life this day."

## Chapter 35

Jemma, with canvas in hand, opened the kitchen door and hailed, "Good afternoon, ladies! So good to be home again!" Melissa, open-mouthed like a nestling, was in her highchair, and Catherine was scooping into the child spoons full of what appeared to be carrots, peas, and rice cereal with applesauce.

"Hello, dear," Catherine responded without interrupting the cadence of her feeding. "This child eats in direct proportion to whatever is set before her." Holding up the child's pudgy arm, she added, "Hopefully, she will stretch out these rolls when she starts walking and gaining height.

Jemma squeezed Missy's cheeks and gave her a kiss on the nose. "Hey, sweet baby. I missed you."

"What have you got there?" Catherine asked, pointing with baby spoon in hand.

"Let me show you." Slipping the wrapping off, without comment, she set the portrait on the table.

"Oh, Jemma, that is absolutely the most … well … it just captures everything about Melissa. It's wonderful! I assume Keeton Fox did it."

"Yes, it's beyond special—a real treasure. I know Uncle Virgil will be completely captivated by it."

"He's in the living room. He's been resting while waiting on you. He wants to hear how your day went at the office. We're going to do some shopping if you want to go with us. More snow is expected overnight, and we need to restock."

"I think we're in good shape—Melissa has plenty of food and formula, and I've got soups and frozen dinners—healthy ones, mind you," she nodded. "Besides, all-wheel drive will get us where we need to go, and the Subaru is loaded with emergency supplies. I hope you don't mind, but I'm going to let Missy spend some time at day care tomorrow. She needs to be around other children a little more—maybe work off some of those rolls … though precious is each and every one," she added, tickling the baby's knee.

Jemma found her uncle stretched out before the fireplace and greeted him: "Uncle Virgil, I have something exquisite to show you." He sat up to give attention as she turned the painting toward him to reveal the portrait. She declared, "Melissa Jane Garrison."

Pushing his glasses up the bridge of his nose, he declared, "That is amazing! Keeton has outdone himself. It *is* Fox's work, I assume," he queried.

"Oh, yes, and I've never seen any portrait that better captures the essence of a little one with such clarity. The innocence of the child and the love of the artist for her are apparent. It makes me joyful, but it is bittersweet: Keeton began the sketches when he watched Missy the day Seth fell. I'll think of Seth whenever I look at it, but I will feel nothing but love for the child and for the man."

"Keeton cares for you both a great deal, seems to me."

"I know he looks to me as a friend who will be honestly helpful, and he loves children." Jemma related to Virgil her conversation with Keeton and the unreported background of the newspaper article. She concluded: "I likely would be where Keeton is now, if the relationship with Cory hadn't ended—being used and dumped when something better came along."

"I'm sorry he's having to go through this, but maybe he'll come out of it stronger and wiser. I'll give him a call this week and see if there is any way I can be of help."

"I know he'd appreciate that." Jemma headed toward the office area of her suite. "If you and Aunt Cat can stay here for five more minutes, I'm going to hang this right now. I have the perfect place for it."

Jemma marched to the wall where Keeton's "Two Worlds" was displayed. As lovely as it was, now it spoke to her only of the heartache Kalie had caused. The subject's faint smile was no longer an expression of sadness, regret—whatever; it was a sneer of contempt, unrecognized by an artist prejudiced by love. Jemma removed the painting and, in its place, hung "Melissa." When Missy was no longer with her—though she knew the picture would bring tears for a time—she prayed, ultimately, it would simply bring joy in the sweetness and hope of the baby's innocent life.

As she gazed at the picture, she was pricked by one of those flashes of insight that whizzes through the mind and escapes before one can capture its meaning in memory. Try as she might, she could not remember the thought or its significance. *Well, maybe it'll come back to me.* Picking up "Two Worlds," she pondered: *Now, what am I going to do with this?* She knew the painting was valuable, but she didn't want it. *It's not a good time to ask Keeton about it*, she thought. *Maybe it could be shown online. Someone would surely buy it—someone who knows nothing about its "colorful" background.*

As she moved toward the storage room with the picture of Kalie, she suddenly remembered. She rushed back to the office and held up "Two Worlds" next to "Melissa." Was it an illusion … maybe the similar racial identity … was her mind playing a cruel trick? "Uncle Virgil," she called. "Can you come in here, please?"

"Need some help?" he asked as he walked into the room.

"Come here, please, and tell me what you see. Look carefully."

Virgil studied the paintings—each one, up closely, intently; then, he stepped back and viewed them as a pair. "I think I know what you're suggesting."

"And that is?" she prodded.

"There is a resemblance—but then, they're both Native American. There would be similarities between them."

"Yes, I suppose you're right," she hesitated. "But look at the eyes, the mouth … even that slight cleft of chin."

"What are you proposing?"

"What if Keeton's wife told him she got rid of the baby, but it was not what he assumed—she did not abort the baby but abandoned the baby?"

"How would anyone ever know?"

"I've got to find Kalie Fox and ask her," Jemma declared.

"Jemma, maybe you just need to stay out of this. You don't know what you might be getting into. There's that other man involved now, and you don't know what kind of person he may be."

"Yes, but Uncle Virgil, just think: If Melissa is Kalie's baby and Keeton is the father—with her lifestyle, that likely would have to be proven by DNA—but, if Keeton is her father, Melissa would be legally his—she would go to him. She would be loved and safe, and she would not be lost to us. He might even let her stay with us when he had to make trips out of town. The tribe would be content—they respect Keeton, and he could teach her about the heritage and culture of that world, while giving her the advantages of living in this one."

Virgil shook his head, "I don't know, Jemma. Stranger coincidences have occurred, I guess." He paused, then, with hope in his voice, he asked, "What do we do?"

She thought for a moment. "Kalie told Keeton she got a divorce in Sheridan. That would be a matter of public record. Wouldn't there be a local address in a file somewhere?"

"Tomorrow I'll check with Abrams, my attorney—Stella's husband. This kind of thing is not his field, but he'll know how to get the information."

## Chapter 36

Jemma surveyed the shipment of new spring merchandise that would go on the racks and shelves even before the Christmas sales were finished. She had experienced marketing from the customer's side, but she was surprised she found the retailer's involvement so interesting, even exciting. She had to admit she enjoyed the Western apparel, the styles, the colors—and being able to pull and purchase items before they were available to the general public. Maybe that wasn't entirely fair, but there were few shoppers who required size eleven boots and extra-length women's pants and shirt sleeves. She was learning all she could about the saddlery and ranch supplies side of the business but, *This side's a cinch*. She smiled at the pun, remembering the previous one about an artist's typically "colorful" background.

Jemma felt energized this morning and prepared to confront Kalie Fox. She would get to the truth. And, if that clear image she had constructed in her mind was the truth, there could be a right and just outcome for all involved. She was wondering if Uncle Virgil had been able to contact his attorney to get Kalie's location, when her cell rang, and the I. D. indicated it was Stella Abrams. "Good morning, Stella," she answered.

"Good morning, Jemma. I hope you are well," came the perfunctory greeting.

"Yes. You, too."

"Jemma, my husband Richard told me about your uncle's call and request for Kalie Fox's location. The background information was very interesting. I'd like to advise you to let me handle this in my position as

Melissa's social worker. I know you are an intelligent, level-headed woman, who would not want to pursue this without valid suspicion she may be connected to Melissa. I have the address she gave in the divorce documentation. If I can get her phone number, I'll call and arrange a meeting; if not, I'll just make an unscheduled visit to this address.

"When I locate her, I'll tell her we have received information she may have given birth and abandoned a child at the hospital about seven months ago—and, we have proof the child is not Hispanic, as she said. Kalie needs to know the Tribal Council has made a claim on the baby and to understand that the child may be taken from foster care and placed with a biological relative—perhaps, even an abusive grandfather. I'll assure her there will be no legal action against her if she confirms the allegation and gives us the name of the father, the rightful guardian. Also, I will tell her paternity may be proved by DNA matching—not that we would do that, you know, but just to pressure her to tell the truth.

"Also, we will keep this a private matter. We don't want to give Keeton Fox false hope with awareness of our inquiry—or to upset him by learning his wife gave birth to another man's child. From what I understand, he's going through enough."

Jemma's response was thoughtful, deliberate: "Yes, he is, Stella. I believe he hit bottom in that moment when he literally threw Kalie out the door, but he wants a new start. And again, thank you. You are right. This is the wise and proper course."

"And, Jemma, just between us, I might have to imply—if she did abandon Melissa—that she'll not face consequences if the charge against Keeton is dismissed. Further legal proceedings would bring out in court the full, sordid context of the 'disorderly conduct.' A mother who said she 'got rid' of her baby by abandonment would be a stain on even her shady character."

Jemma asked, "If she claims Keeton is the father, what kind of legal proceedings will there be?"

"I'm not sure. We would contact the attorney for the Tribal Council to tell him what we have learned and to let him know it appears the father is a member of the tribe in good standing. The parental rights of the father must be reinstated—that should be no problem; he had no knowledge of the baby. At some point, a new birth certificate would be issued, naming Keeton Fox as the father and rightful guardian. This, obviously, is an unusual case, but it would seem one easily resolved if and when the true father is aware and receptive."

"Stella, I just really feel this is right. To me, Melissa is a miniature version of Kalie Fox. Keeton has not indicated he sees any resemblance, but perhaps, he has a special fondness for Melissa because she does remind him of Kalie. He wouldn't necessarily relate that to Kalie's possibly being her mother. Melissa seems to be drawn to Keeton, too." She laughed: "He says that's because he's the only one in her small world who has dark hair and eyes like her Teddy bear. Maybe it's my fanciful imagination and wanting to keep Melissa close, but I think—I pray, God has His hand in working this out."

"Well, Jemma, just pray and stay close. From here on, this will be Social Services' business. You won't be in the loop during the investigation. I'm not sure what the proceeding will be if Melissa's parentage is confirmed, but I'll try to let you know if all is well. Since Melissa is still in your foster care, you might be asked to be in court at some point. If you should receive a summons, just be there."

"Stella, thanks again, for trusting me and being willing to follow what may lead to a dead end."

"No need to thank me. Melissa is my child, too, in a way. I want what's best for her. If there is a chance …"

Jemma interrupted: "Only in games, Stella. I believe in prayer and providence, especially when a child like Missy is involved. Maybe I landed in Wyoming, at the hospital, in the NICU, to help a little girl find her rightful place in this world. I've been looking for my purpose, and maybe it was something as simple—and as momentous as that."

## Chapter 37

Patience was not Jemma's strong suit, but she had plenty to keep her distracted while waiting to hear something from Stella. Laurie and Stan's wedding would be the week before Thanksgiving, and they had called to tell her they were flying to Wyoming for their honeymoon. *Glad they're not "beach bums,"* she mused. Their parents, Charles and Rita, would be a couple of days behind them—and, if convenient, they all would like to be in Sheridan for Thanksgiving. That was only a few weeks away, and Jemma prayed not only for passable weather, but that Melissa would still be at Garrison House.

It had not been a week since her communication with Stella, and she was trying to lose her concern in the responsibilities at the Emporium and in the joy of her role as Beta Mom, as temporary as that might be. Melissa lay sleeping in her lap after her evening bottle, and Jemma delayed putting her in the crib, not wanting to give up the moment of peace and contentment, the sweet baby powder smell, and the softness of the small pudgy body in her lap. As she continued to rock, Jemma thought, *Before long this house could be full of laughter with Missy tricycling down halls.* Jemma imagined an older Melissa trying to slide down the banister of the grand staircase and finding places to conceal "treasures" in the "hidey-holes" of the attic. *What a great house for growing up and making childhood memories! How lonely it would be without her!*

Then came another insight—more neurons firing: *This house is really too much for one person or even a couple without children ... but a school ... maybe even a boarding school—a girls' school. We could easily house, maybe, six to eight older girls upstairs in the apartment, and the nursery could be reworked to hold around six younger ones. We probably wouldn't want to deal with more than that number, at least initially. "Garrison Academy" ... that just sounds right.* Jemma's mind began whirring with possibilities. The problem with private schooling is typically the cost. But it would be non-profit, and the Emporium could provide an endowment; she knew the business was strong and stable financially and could use the tax advantages. *Teachers? What about Stan and Laurie? They're already in the profession and, obviously, love this area. The Tribal Council might even allow us to give a couple of scholarships to children of the Nation— perhaps those seeking advanced degrees who might need intensive college prep.*

*On a personal, selfish level,* she thought with a smile of satisfaction, *if Keeton regains custody of Melissa, he might allow her to be a full-time boarding student. I'll have to check the legal procedures and requirements, but this just might work.* Jemma knew her aunt and uncle could get excited about such an "air castle" and would want to be involved. *The students would be filled with cinnamon rolls on a daily basis,* she laughed to herself.

Reluctantly Jemma put Melissa in her crib and covered her with her "Pooh" blanket. Jemma needed to make a list of Thanksgiving preparations, of course, but she also wanted to see if she could get information online about setting up a private school in the State of Wyoming. The thought flashed through her mind: *Bet it's not as easy and quick as getting a divorce!*

Jemma had researched online for hours and had made several pages of notes when weariness began shutting down her faculties. She did learn the private school must be considered a "religious" institution, or their small staff would be continually jumping through State regulatory hoops. Nearly all the staff she had in mind would have a common foundation of faith: Uncle Virgil could teach Bible history, and Laurie could teach the Bible as literature. Among their church family, they might locate others qualified to handle certain subjects on a full or part-time basis. The primary goal, she believed, would be to give students not only a strong academic foundation, but also a "rock-solid" faith, confidence in having a place from which to "launch," and security in knowing it was also a place on which to land and bounce back when life's trials and troubles knocked them down.

Jemma prayed that Keeton might find and develop such a launching and landing pad in the months ahead—when he got legs of faith beneath him, maybe he could teach some art classes … or local history and culture of the Apsaalooke. She lay her head on the cushiony softness of her lavender-scented pillow and wondered if she would dream—and of what … or if she would wake and regret the time and energy she had wasted this night. She turned off the bedside lamp, remembering, *I never made that Thanksgiving list!*

# Chapter 38

"Good morning, Uncle Virgil. How are you and Aunt Cat today?" Jemma asked, holding her phone on her shoulder against her ear as she prepared her coffee.

"We're 'up and at 'em,'" he responded cheerily, "on our feet since six. This is an early hour for you, isn't it?"

Jemma responded: "Melissa will be waking up soon, so I thought I'd get ahead of her—fix breakfast and pack her food and bottles. Today's her day with Catherine."

"And with me, too," he corrected.

"Yes, and with you, too," she laughed. But I'd like for you to spend some time with me —maybe over a bison burger at lunch. I've got a lot on my mind, particularly an idea I'd like to discuss. I've had it ballooning in my mind for a time—you'll know if you need to bring me back down to earth."

"Oh, boy, one of those ideas—with an expenditure of time, talent, or resources—or, likely, all three."

"Bingo! Want to meet me at the office at noon? We can walk up to the burger shop and talk ideas and then come back to the office to talk shop. You might want to check out a few changes I've made here and there in the store."

"Sounds like a plan. I'll see you when you bring Missy over. Love you!"

"Love you both, too!"

Jemma was just taking Melissa's coat from the rack near the kitchen door when her cell rang, and she saw with excitement and apprehension that it was Stella.

"Jemma, this is Stella Abrams. I want to inform you of a hearing before Judge Riley Hendricks Thursday morning at nine. He would like you to be there with Melissa. Will that be a problem?"

"The day after tomorrow Thursday?" Jemma asked.

"Yes, that's right. Courtroom 2 in the County Court House. Do you know where that is?"

"Yes … I do. Do I need an attorney?"

"No, no, your presence is all that's required. Roger Burnham will be there, and I will be representing Melissa as her caseworker."

"Will it be all right if Uncle Virgil and Aunt Catherine are with us? I'd like their support," Jemma asked. She tried to sound calm, though her pulse was racing.

"That would be fine—it's an open hearing. The public is allowed."

"Okay …"

"Jemma, I'll confirm the time, date, and location. Be sure and check your messages."

"I will. Thank you, Stella." The line went silent.

Again, Jemma reached to take the outerwear from the rack. Her message notification sounded, she punched the icon, and Stella's message appeared at the top of the screen: "Please appear Thursday, November 3, 9:00 A. M., Courtroom 2, District Court, County Court House."

Following the information was simply a "thumbs up" icon—a large one, and Jemma smiled.

Jemma placed Melissa's bags on the table and began to remove the baby's coat and mittens. Uncle Virgil immediately captured the freed child and hugged her to his face to kiss her cheek. "I have what I think is good news." Jemma was excited: "We have a court hearing Thursday at nine, and we all can be there. I have no idea what it's about, but Stella gave me a big "thumbs up" message—probably more information than she should have—but all seems to be positive."

"Oh, that's wonderful news!" Catherine exclaimed. "We'll be there, hoping and praying for the best."

"And the best will be that this little girl will be in our lives as long as we have them," added Virgil."

"Well, I'll be trusting in the power of prayer and the positive import of the thumbs-up emoji," Jemma laughed.


"It's been nearly two weeks since I last had a bison burger," Virgil declared. "I've missed this place. Don't get me wrong—Catherine is the greatest cook in the world, but doing without bison burgers has nearly had me in withdrawal."

"Uncle Virgil! If you're that addicted to them, maybe you ought to give them up for good—go into rehab or something," she teased.

"No, the Scriptures are silent on the subject of bison burgers—and I never make a glutton of myself, so I just enjoy every bite."

"Well, since you referred to your spiritual knowledge …" Jemma launched into her thoughts about establishing the private religious school, "Garrison Academy." She reviewed the notes she had made from her online research and added, "I had thought about a boarding school for girls, but that would require more staff and expense. Perhaps, it could be a coed academy for children who are motivated and eager to learn—perhaps, even give scholarships for some from the reservation. But, of course, they would need housing. Oh, I don't know—do you have any thoughts about it?"

Virgil paused, as he finished his last bite and wiped the napkin across his mouth. "I find the idea interesting—appealing, especially giving children from the reservation scholarships. My initial thought is, yes, make it a boarding school for girls, where those who want to prepare for college can come and develop their potential academically, while growing spiritually and in good moral character. We might prevent another Kalie Fox … though I'm thankful for the child she produced."

"That would be rewarding. I'd like to talk with Laurie and Stan about it when they come for Thanksgiving. They would be outstanding teachers, extremely well-qualified and credentialed. We'd have a great start on staffing if they had serious interest in the project. But they'd have to have incomes—and they'll be growing a family in the coming years."

"Jemma, don't be concerned about the financial part of it. I have friends, investors, properties, and bank accounts. We may have to limit scholarship enrollment, at least for a few years. And we can set a fair schedule of tuition and fees for parents who can afford to pay. But if Laurie and Stan are interested, they can determine what they'd need to move here and set up residence. If Garrison Academy becomes a reality, their salaries will be there."

## Chapter 39

The Garrisons entered the courthouse and passed through the metal detector before proceeding down the hall to the courtroom. Police officers stood on guard, as attorneys, court clerks, and other personnel obviously involved in proceedings scurried from doorway to doorway along the corridor. The "public," of which they were a part, filled the few benches and stood against the walls waiting for the doors of Courtroom 2 to open.

Melissa was wary and resisted the attention of the people who passed, some of them stopping to speak to the "pretty little baby." When Missy threatened to cry, Jemma searched in the diaper bag for a pacifier. "Here, let me help," she heard a voice say, and she looked up into the face of Keeton Fox. He reached for Melissa, who came to him and immediately stopped whimpering.

"Oh, Keeton, thank you. She's uncomfortable with all these strangers around her."

"I received a summons to be here this morning. Do you know why we are here? Why are *you* here?"

"I really don't know. Like you, I got a message from Stella Abrams that we were summoned to be in court this morning." Jemma was glad she knew no details.

They stood in patient silence while waiting for Courtroom 2 to open. Then the Garrisons and Keeton Fox filed in with the rest of the public and filled most of the first row behind the attorneys' tables. To their right sat Roger Burnham and Stella Abrams, and to their left, they assumed, sat two lawyers representing the Tribal Council.

The bailiff entered shortly after everyone was settled. "All rise. This court with the Honorable Judge

Riley Hendricks presiding is now in session. Please be seated and come to order."

"Good morning, ladies and gentlemen," the judge greeted warmly. Our first order of business today has been settled, for the most part, in my chambers. We have a series of petitions, charges, a dismissal, and some general housekeeping we need to attend to concerning a most interesting case, unique in my experience on the bench. Because the circumstances of the case cross state lines, I have been granted the authority to announce judgments of other jurisdictions and to make a final decree on pertinent matters.

"First," he continued, "all charges of domestic disorderly conduct against Keeton Fox have been dismissed in Yellowstone County, Montana."

Keeton grabbed Jemma's hand and dropped his face onto the dark curls of Melissa.

"Next, Mr. Pease, I believe you have a statement."

"Yes, your honor. As legal representative of the Apsaalooke Tribal Council, I withdraw the petition for custody of the child known as Melissa Garrison."

Jemma's heart was pounding with surprise and excitement.

"Thank you, Mr. Pease. Mr. Burnham?"

"As the attorney representing Miss Jemma Garrison, I withdraw her petition for custody of the child known as Melissa Garrison. The biological father has been located. He was unaware of the child's birth but is able and will be willing to take full and responsible custody of his daughter. Of course, we will be seeking to have his rights reinstated and to have a new birth certificate issued declaring Keeton Fox as the rightful and legal father of the child in question."

Virgil, sitting on the other side of Keeton, took

Melissa into his arms, so that Keeton could give full vent to his emotions and weeping. Jemma pulled tissues from the diaper bag, handed some to Keeton, and shared the rest, as needed, with those around her.

"Is that all you have, Mr. Burnham?"

"Yes, your honor."

"Mr. Pease?"

"Yes, your honor."

"Well, this court is pleased that this little girl is going to have the love and care not only of her father, but of this family of friends. My best wishes for her and for you all."

With the sound of the gavel, they were dismissed.

When they entered the hallway and the court door closed behind them, Virgil announced, "Keeton, here's your little girl" and transferred Melissa into her father's arms.

"My child," he stated, cupping the small face in his hand. Turning to Jemma, he asked, "Did you know?"

"No," she answered. "But I suspected, and Stella and Roger Burnham trusted my intuition. Have you not seen Kalie's likeness in your daughter's face?"

"Yes … but I thought it was just my eyes seeing through some sort of emotional filter. I have felt a connection to this child since that day in the bookstore, when you had that cart full of baby books and CDs," he laughed. Burying his face in Missy's hair, he said, "You are going to be such a smart little girl with Jemma as your teacher." He looked at Jemma with fatherly concern and asked, "Can we keep the living circumstances the same until I can make some changes in my place?"

Virgil answered for his niece: "Surely, Keeton, Garrison House will always be a home for Melissa."

Keeton declared: "She is now my responsibility, in every way. But I'd like to work out an arrangement where she could live with you much of the time—I often need long hours uninterrupted in a project, and sometimes I must travel."

Jemma nudged her uncle. "We'd have like a boarding school situation?"

"Yes, exactly," Keeton answered.

"I think that would be an excellent arrangement," Jemma declared.

# Chapter 40

"Dad, Catherine and I are taking the turkey out of the oven. Can you get the door?" Jemma called to her father.

"What do you want me to do with it when I get it?"

"Dad, please, be serious. Just get the door—and remember your manners," she cautioned.

"Good morning … and 'Happy Thanksgiving!'" he greeted, opening the door to Keeton and his father. The men knocked the snow off their boots on the porch, before removing them and placing them on the mat inside the door. Charles extended his hand to a handsome, graying Native American man about his age: "I'm Charles Garrison, Jemma's father, and then to Keeton: "Good to see you again."

"And you, too," Keeton responded. "This is my father, Joseph Whitefox."

"Mr. Whitefox, thank you for joining us."

"Call me 'Joe.'"

"And I'm 'Charlie.'"

Joe Whitefox looked around the room at the others assembled there—Virgil, Rita, Stan, and Laurie. "What, no Pilgrim costumes?"

"Dad!" Keeton grinned and shook his head.

For a moment there was silence in the room, and he asked Charles, "Don't they get the joke?"

Then laughter spurted, and Charles slapped him on the back. "Joe, a man after my own heart! Come … meet the family."

Jemma and Catherine entered the room to greet their guests. "Mr. Whitefox, I'm so pleased you could join us," Jemma said. Turning to Catherine, she added, "This is my

Aunt Catherine, Uncle Virgil's wife." Catherine smiled and nodded, "Welcome."

"Need any help, Catherine?" Rita asked.

"Well, if you girls will check the table settings and fill the water glasses—make sure everything we need is on the table, then we can start placing the serving dishes on the sideboard," she answered.

"Will do," Laurie agreed, as she stood up, releasing Stan's hand and saying to him affectionately, "Back soon."

Rita called, "Mr. Whitefox, would you like to come and take your granddaughter? I don't think I can stand up with this extra eighteen pounds in my arms."

Without answering, Joe moved to take the child, who smiled at her grandfather in response to his "Kaheé, Melissa. He looked at Rita and explained, "Hello."

"You know, Joe, you people like a lot of letters in your words," Charlie observed. "Some of the highway signs around here can barely contain one place name, and that's all squished together."

"Squished? Hmm … don't know that English word," he winked. "And, if you notice," Joe explained, "they're mostly vowels. We're really fond of lots of vowels."

Charles laughed, "Have a seat, Joe." He motioned to the twin armchairs in front of the fire. "Keeton, please, get comfortable. I look forward to talking to both of you sometime about local history—that's my avocation. The Garrisons go back a long way in this area, and it's interesting to think little Melissa has brought our families together."

Virgil waited for a lull in the communication between his nephew and Joe Whitefox to speak: "Before you two get into any lengthy discussion—or reenact Custer's Last Stand, I have something I want to say to Keeton."

"Yes, Virgil?"

"Keeton, I am so happy things worked out as they did—not only for you, but for us. We love Melissa and are thankful to be included among the friends and family who will watch her grow up—to take her place in your world and in ours. I pray she has only the best of both." He continued, "And thank you for keeping her name—I've become so accustomed to it, she'll always be Melissa Jane. 'Melissa Jane Whitefox' is a name with dignity and beauty."

Joe agreed, "Yes, 'dignity and beauty.' Women are very important in our nation. They may hold positions of honor and respect—even becoming chiefs and warriors in the past." He continued, "Sadly, the modern world has crept into our reservation and influenced many of our young women, who have not acted in ways worthy of their heritage."

"Dad, let's don't get into that on a day of celebration like today," Keeton advised.

"Yes, my son, you are right." Turning to Charles, "You know, Charlie, a reenactment would be interesting, but not very productive—same outcome every time. I lost an ancestor, a scout, in the conflict, though, ultimately, our enemy, the Lakota, were defeated— and we did get the land. 'You win some, you lose some,' as the saying goes— though Custer never said it after Little Bighorn."

The men joined in laughter, interrupted by Catherine, who came to take Melissa from Joe's arms while directing: "If you will go to the dining room and find your places, we'll give thanks for the food, and then you men can serve your plates at the sideboard. Virgil, you'll say the prayer?"

"Yes, dear." He escorted the men to the long table, around which the upholstered dining chairs stood ready to accommodate each person with plenty of elbow and eating room.

Taking his place at the head of the table and directing Joe Whitefox to the opposite end, Virgil said: "Let's give thanks. Our gracious Giver and Receiver of life, we come before You as family and friends joined in love and peace with one another. We thank You for the bounty we have before us and for this day of celebration that calls us to remember and to be grateful for the blessings that make it possible. We pray for the health of our bodies and for the strength of our minds to seek You and Your will for our lives. May we always remember it is to You we should give glory and honor by the way in which we live and move through our time in this world. In the name of the Savior, we pray. Amen."

Joe Whitefox spoke up: "Before we serve our food, I'd like to say, 'Congratulations and Best Wishes' to Stan and Laurie. And I am reminded of some words: 'When we gladly eat our daily bread, we bless the Hand that feeds us; And when we tread the road of Life in cheerfulness, our very heart-beats praise the Love that leads us.'"

Charlie asked, "Crow?"

Joe picked up his plate and said, "No, white man, Henry Van Dyke."

The laughter faded as the men moved toward the sideboard to fill their plates. While Catherine fed Melissa in the kitchen, Rita and Laurie started tidying the countertops while waiting for the men to be seated. Jemma stood in attendance at the kitchen doorway. She thought, *So far this day could not be going any better. I never would have imagined Joe Whitefox to be a dryer, darker version of Dad? Likely the only conflict between these two would be who will upstage the other.*

She remembered Joe's skirting the edge of the

worldliness problem, particularly among the tribe's young women. She could see an obvious entree, at a later date, into discussion about how a school—Garrison Academy, might be beneficial even to their neighbors on the reservation.

Jemma was amazed at how quickly lives and circumstances could change, when those lives and circumstances were in the hands and plans of God. She lowered her eyes and spoke her own private prayer of thanks—for the strength to rise out of ashes, to make new beginnings—for the love of a man like Seth, whose face and words would always have a place in her heart—for family, friends, a home, and blessings to share—and for Melissa Jane Whitefox, who brought two worlds together around this Thanksgiving table.

9 781961 504165